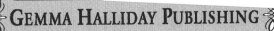

GEMMA HALLIDAY PUBLISHING

MYSTIC MISCHIEF

A Mystic Isle
Mystery
· 3 ·

USA TODAY BESTSELLING AUTHORS
Sally J. Smith &
Jean Steffens

BOOKS BY SALLY J. SMITH & JEAN STEFFENS

Mystic Isle Mysteries:
Mystic Mayhem
Mystic Mojo (short story in the Killer Beach Reads collection)
Mystic Mistletoe Murder
Mystic Mischief

Danger Cove Pet Sitter Mysteries:
Passion, Poison & Puppy Dogs
Divas, Diamonds & Death

Aloha Lagoon Mysteries:
Murder on the Aloha Express

MYSTIC MISCHIEF

a Mystic Isle mystery

Sally J. Smith & Jean Steffens

The authors wish to thank Wendi Baker for her hard work and guidance in maintaining continuity and tying up loose ends (God knows we need it). Also, our thanks go out to Kristin Huston for her careful copy edits, as well as to Janet Holmes who continues to amaze us with her charming cover art.

To Denise, Dan, and Tom. Thanks for your loving support and encouragement. —Jean

Mystic Mischief is for my sweet pirate wench, Carrie Sue. Yo-ho, yo-ho. —Sally

CHAPTER ONE

———

I was grumpy.

I was airsick.

And I was going crazy at about five hundred miles per hour.

Grumpy, airsick, crazy—and we were still an hour away from landing in New Orleans.

Crazy because we got stuck sitting in the back of the plane where a high school glee club was seated en masse. They'd been singing their little hearts out from the minute we were wheels up. It was to the point where if I heard one more chorus of "You Can't Stop the Beat"—complete with clapping, snapping, and hand choreography—I might have to ask for a parachute.

Airsick because our Delta flight from Palm Beach to New Orleans was rough. A late-season tropical storm had whipped up off the Gulf Coast of Florida and stayed with us all the way to our stopover in Atlanta. We were now on the last leg of our trip back to New Orleans. Jack Stockton, my boss and boyfriend, was weathering the dips and drops much better than I was. Having to keep the airsick bag close at hand never made for a great flight.

And lastly, I was *grumpy* because my introductory visit to Jack's parents in Florida couldn't have gone much worse. The air tickets had been Jack's Christmas gift to me, and I'd been so excited to meet his folks.

But Jack's mother was standoffish from that first awkward moment at their front door when I had gone in to hug her and she ducked away, presenting her hand for a cool shake. It had gotten so bad that when I couldn't take the cold shoulder any longer, I'd begged Jack to cut the trip short and fly home with me three days early. He had, and I was at least grateful for that.

I'd tried my best not to be childish about it and take it out on him. Jack couldn't help it if his mother was the Wicked Witch of the West, but from my point of view, he could at least have stood up more for me. Her little innuendoes about my less-than-desirable background and inappropriate profession were hurtful. And when Jack's old girlfriend Sydney had shown up for Mrs. Stockton's dinner party, good old Elphaba had seated the two of them together. And where was I? At the other end of the table beside Jack's dad—who, by the way, was funny and real, a sweetheart of a guy.

Mr. Stockton kept apologizing, and so did Jack, but neither one of them called her on the carpet for the snub—at least not in front of me. Jack swore he'd taken her aside and asked her to cool it, but I never saw it, and I'm a "show me" kind of girl. Besides, if he did ask, she'd ignored him.

As the wannabe cast of *Glee* rolled into yet another round of the song from *Hairspray*, I plugged in my earbuds to listen to the monitor in front of me, immediately recognizing an up-and-coming New Orleans boy wonder from one of the local TV stations. He was broadcasting from outside, and the area behind him looked an awful lot like the bayou near The Mansion at Mystic Isle where Jack and I both worked—Jack as the resort's general manager and I, Melanie Hamilton, as the resident tattoo artist. Yes. That was what I said, *a resort that employed a tattoo artist*.

But that wasn't as off the wall as it sounded. The Mansion at Mystic Isle wasn't like any other resort—that I knew of, anyway. The place was solely dedicated to fans of the supernatural, paranormal, and other offbeat, often-creepy elements. My job was to design otherworldly tattoos that would help resort guests commemorate their visit to Mystic Isle—our patrons were understandably not the kind of travelers who'd be content to pick up a refrigerator magnet or a couple of postcards in the gift shop.

I turned up the volume so I could hear what the TV reporter had to say over twenty kids in four-part harmony.

The handsome creole, teeth gleaming, spoke into a handheld mic. "This is Etienne Charles reporting from Barataria Preserve in the heart of the Louisiana Bayou. With me are Archie and Theresa Powell, archeologists, dealers of antiquities, and all-around adventurers."

The reporter turned to a tall man who looked to be in his late forties or early fifties. He wore a battered fedora that I could have sworn I'd once seen on an Indiana Jones poster, along with the khaki cargo shorts and a short-sleeved shirt you'd have expected to see on safari. His face was long, his features unremarkable and a tad washed out and colorless. His eyes and mouth turned down so that even if he were smiling, I doubted he'd look happy.

Beside the man a much younger willowy brunette with flashing dark eyes and a haughty expression had struck a red-carpet pose. An army green tank top stretched across impressive breasts, the kind some plastic surgeon had sacrificed fifteen years of his youth to learn how to construct. Her tight low-riding shorts were belted with a utility band sheathing a knife with a handle that looked to be at least seven inches. I didn't even want to think about the length of the blade.

The reporter went on. "I understand you've brought a film crew to document your search for Lafitte's presidential pardon—a historical document that's just recently come to light."

Archie Powell took hold of the mic and pulled it toward himself. "Yes, that's right, Etienne. Two young men claiming to be descendants of an out of wedlock relationship between the privateer Jean Lafitte and a mixed-race slave known as Belle Villars recently located the woman's journal. In it she claimed that when Lafitte jilted her, she stole the original letter from him and hid it here in the bayou."

The hot tamale in the tank top took over. "A document of such historical significance would certainly put a feather in the cap of anyone who'd be lucky enough to locate it." She batted her eyes and cast a sideways glance at the studly young reporter. "Don't you think so, Etienne?"

Jack was awake and lobbing over into my space to get a look at the screen. He pulled one of my earbuds loose. "That looks like the grounds near The Mansion."

"They're in the preserve." My tone was so frosty, wine would have chilled to perfection on that statement. "Something about a lost document."

"And they think it's at Mystic Isle?"

I sighed so Jack wouldn't mistake my irritation then switched the earbuds around so we could share them.

Archie was speaking again. "Evidently the document never left the Villars plantation—the plantation currently incarnated as a resort, The Mansion at Mystic Isle."

The reporter was positively leering at the woman. "So, Mrs. Powell—"

"Theresa, please." I was pretty sure she was purring.

"Theresa." He corrected himself. "You've come all the way to our little corner of the world to try to beat the Villars family, the brothers who own this so-called journal, in locating the document?"

One corner of Mrs. Powell's full lips curved in a half smile. She nodded slowly, almost lazily, and laid one elegant hand on the hilt of that knife, caressing it. "That's right, Etienne."

Even on the small back-of-the-seat monitor, the reporter's fluster in the presence of such sensuality was evident. Etienne turned to the camera. "We asked to interview Elroy and Percy Villars and their sister, who've brought the mysterious journal to the bayou to look for Lafitte's letter. So far, they've declined to appear." The reporter turned and graced his viewers with an engaging grin. "Wow, folks. Sounds sort of like a rousing game of *Tomb Raider*, doesn't it?" He ran a finger around the collar of his shirt. "I know I, for one, can't wait to see what happens."

Jack let the earbud drop and leaned back in his seat, laying his hand on top of mine. "Huh," he said. "That's kinda cool, isn't it? What do you think, Mel? This ought to stir up a little excitement and some new business for the resort."

"Probably."

He cocked his head and smiled. It was nearly my undoing or at least the undoing of my bad mood. Jack's smile was like the break of dawn. It lit up his whiskey-colored eyes.

I pulled my hand off the armrest and out from under his. "Don't think you're off the hook yet, Stockton. I'm still sore at you." The truth was, I was more hurt than angry, but opening my chest to bare my heart and let him know how wounded I'd been over his mother's rebuffs would have made me too emotional, too vulnerable—not something I was in the mood for on a crowded airplane.

We landed almost twenty minutes late at Louis Armstrong New Orleans International Airport. It was a rainy and chilly fall night—matched my mood perfectly.

CHAPTER TWO

———

I spent the night with Jack at his cute little cottage at the back of the resort. I'd been staying with him the last few weeks since Quincy, my roommate's fiancé, a Chief Deputy in the Jefferson Parrish Sheriff's Department, had moved into our place to plan their upcoming wedding and (something I thought was brilliant) talk and plan about what they each expected from their married life.

Even though my back had been to Jack all night, Jack had been calm and nonconfrontational, even seeming to understand what I was feeling. And by Saturday morning the weather had cleared up, and so had my attitude, that was, until I walked into the resort lobby to see Sydney Baxter, who'd been introduced to me by Jack's mother as "the one who Jack let slip through his fingers," apparently checking in. Well, that was certainly fast. Seeing Jack and me together must have triggered something in her—the urge to try for another shot at him or, at the very least, some vagabond itch to travel to the Louisiana bayou.

Lurch, our monolithic seven-foot-tall doorman, stood stoically by, balancing two large and two smaller suitcases while Sydney chatted with Lucy, the front desk receptionist.

Sydney finished and turned around, her blonde curls bouncing, her tiny hands applauding, little girl feet in knee-high black patent boots shuffling in excitement as she squealed, "Oh my good gracious, will you look at that." She took two steps to Lurch's side, her head coming only to his chest, and put one hand on his bicep. "You big strong man, you."

An unintelligible rumble came from Lurch. It sounded like a waste management truck on a wooden bridge. Then, to my amazement, he flexed his arm, still holding the two big suitcases in a hand the size of a tennis racket head. His normally grim countenance creased in a rare smile—at least I thought it was a smile. It wasn't a pretty sight. Was Lurch actually flirting with the petite blonde? Eww.

As Sydney led Lurch away and up the stairs to the second floor, it occurred to me that if she brought four suitcases with her, she probably was planning an extended stay. Exactly what the heck was she doing here anyway? I didn't want to dwell on the most likely answer to that question.

Before I jumped to a conclusion that would really piss me off, I needed to talk to Jack. But first I had to go to work, so I made my way to my dominion in the auxiliary wing of the resort and planned to check in with him when I took a break in my morning schedule.

I had three appointments scheduled at Dragons and Deities Tattoo Parlor—one in the morning, two in the afternoon. I turned on some mood music, which consisted of my rather specific playlist—the theme from the Harry Potter films, "Crystal Blue Persuasion," the *Star Trek* theme (the Kirk and Spock version, of course), "Aquarius," even "Love Potion No. 9"—and checked my ink guns. Since it was my first day back after my disastrous trip to Florida, I went down the hall where my best friend and roommate, Catalina Gabor, the resort's tarot card reader, worked at House of Cards.

Cat was exotic-looking, absolutely stunning, a DNA gift from her Romanian ancestors. I stood in the doorway watching her delicate use of a feather duster look like *Swan Lake*, wondering exactly how she managed to be so graceful and beautiful even while doing the most mundane chore.

She looked up and saw me. "Mel!" Her big brown eyes flashed as she threw down the duster, covered the distance between us in a few quick strides, and grabbed me into a hug. "I'm so glad you're back." She pushed back, holding me at arms' length. "Tell me everything! How was your trip to Florida? What were his folks like? Did you have a great time? Are you glad to be home?"

I took a deep breath. "I—"

"I have so much to tell you. The wedding plans are driving me crazy, and Quincy is worse than no help at all. Oh, and you won't believe the gorgeous water feature Harry Villars is having built out back in the garden by the pool, and we're going to have the ceremony out there. I'm just so glad Daddy's being so generous with his money for the wedding. It makes me feel real good to be able to spend it here at the resort, and—" She stopped abruptly and laughed. Then she took hold of both my hands, smiled sweetly, and said in a quiet voice. "Hi, Mel. Welcome home. Can you tell I missed you?"

And it was my turn to laugh. "Makes me feel wanted," I said.

"Okay, one thing at a time. Tell me about Florida."

I frowned. "It could have gone better. But it's a long story we should save to share over a glass of wine. Or two. Or three."

"Oh no." She laid a hand on my arm. "I can tell by the look on your face it was a disappointment."

"You can say that again. And it looks like we brought a haint back with us."

She cocked her head to one side? "A haint? How's that?"

"Yep, a haint by the name of Sydney Baxter. One of Jack's old girlfriends showed up here this morning."

"No! What's that all about?"

"That's what I want to know."

"Well, it's obvious we *do* have to talk. You won't believe all the excitement that's been going on around here. TV and film crews. Fortune hunters."

"I saw something about that on the news."

"It's a real tale, one even worthy of Mystic Isle. Illicit lovers, pirates, redemption, broken hearts, revenge. What more could you want?"

"Something about Jean Lafitte, isn't it? And a missing historical document?"

She took a few minutes to reiterate what I'd heard about the letter of pardon on the news report earlier. "And get this." She gestured dramatically and lowered her voice. "One of the twin brothers is missing. Quincy mentioned it yesterday. The other twin and the sister reported it."

"How about that?" I said. "Until the missing person turns up, looks like this is turning into a real Mystic Isle mystery."

CHAPTER THREE

———

My morning appointment was new to me and new to Mystic Isle, a seventy-something lady with reasonably firm skin. Important to a tattoo artist. She identified herself as a geriatric fortune hunter with a psychic connection to Jean Lafitte who'd come to The Mansion at Mystic Isle when she heard about the search for the privateer's missing letter of pardon.

She'd fixed a look on me I thought was meant to be a piercing, steely-eyed stare but actually came off more as a myopic squint. "I'm convinced if I can get my hands on that paper"—she scrubbed her hands together greedily—"the spirit of ol' Lafitte himself will hook up with me. What do you think about that?"

"Uh," I took a minute, trying to come up with something diplomatic. "Sure."

"You know what they're saying, right? 'Bout that crazy gator that's been terrorizing the place?"

I had no idea what she was talking about. "Gator? No. I haven't heard. What are they saying?"

"I've only been here a couple of days, but I hear for the past week this gator's been running around here. They don't ever know where it will show up or when. A few of the resort staff have been assigned to try to corner the thing when it does make an appearance and hold it for the fish and game people. I saw it last night. It's a sight. And people are saying that the ornery critter's channeling Jean Lafitte himself."

Had the old girl lost it? "Really?" I asked.

"You bet."

I didn't want to encourage her, and we did have a tattoo to ink, so I just said, "Interesting." Then I put my hand on her shoulder, coaxing her back into the chair.

For her tattoo she'd chosen one of my favorite designs, a wood sprite in a scanty off-the-shoulder gown whose gossamer wings of purple, fuchsia, and pink were spread wide and graceful. For its location, her thigh. I knew that particular design backwards and forwards. It was one of my own copyrights and a favorite among my female customers.

The older lady, Ethel Sheridan, had pointed to it enthusiastically and cried out, "That's it. That's the one. Looks just like me in my twenties. I was a stripper, you know. And darn good at it too."

Stripper, eh? I made a mental note to take a second look at that particular design.

Throughout her appointment, Ethel had gone on and on about The Mansion at Mystic Isle and its unique place in the resort industry. "I'm a charter member and honorary national board member of Women in Search of Booty, and I plan on recommending this place for our annual international conference next year. And wow. Your salon is the bee's knees."

"Why thank you, Ethel."

Harry had given me a free hand in the design of the studio. I'd gone with a castle motif with flickering wall sconces, stonemasonry wallpaper, and red and gold drapery swags. Everyone seemed to love it.

A tough cookie, Ethel hadn't even needed a short break from the intensity of being inked, left me an incredibly generous tip when we finished, and promised she'd send her friends and "Booty" sisters my way if they needed a "real nice piece of body art."

I had a break around eleven. After hanging my *Back at 1 o'clock* sign on the door, I headed for the Presto-Change-o Room. It was Saturday, and the lunch special was a bowl of crawfish gumbo and a shrimp po' boy for $10.99—a quarter of that with my employee discount. Harry Villars, a Louisiana gentleman of the finest ilk and the resort's owner, was nothing if not generous with his employees. What he asked us to pay for food barely covered the cost of the ingredients, much less dishing it up and serving it. And he didn't have to give us a discount at all.

To get from the tattoo parlor to the Presto-Change-o Room, I had to cross the lobby. Back in the antebellum days when The Mansion was a cotton plantation, the lobby had been a graceful entry hall, a large circular room with a sweeping ornate staircase to the mini-suites and guest rooms on the second floor. I'd always loved the look of it, the rich wood on the walls, the beveled glass panel on the staircase landing. These days, those stairs were navigated by tourists in Bermuda shorts and flip-flops and their rowdy kids in tow, but once it had been elegant ladies in long gowns with voluminous ruffled skirts and men in waistcoats and trousers supported by suspenders.

The idea of a romantic tryst between Jean Lafitte, affectionately known in my hometown as the Pirate of New Orleans, and the beautiful mixed-race slave stirred my imagination. How it must have broken her heart when the dashing pirate left her to take advantage of his amnesty. I was especially sympathetic now that the beautiful morning with the hint of a Southern autumn in the air had brought with it a fly in the ointment—Sydney Baxter.

I was just wondering if I should do anything about the blonde showing up when it happened—something that made me thrust the cutesy little piece of fluff right out of mind.

My head was turned by a scream. I looked in that direction just in time to see a woman vault to the far side of the reception desk. Other shrieks, both men and women, followed as people scattered in several directions.

Survivalists say when you see people in a crowd turning to run, the smart thing to do is follow suit.

But I didn't move—couldn't. I could only stand glued to the spot, mesmerized at the sight of an alligator, at least eight feet long, scuttling in through the double front entry doors, its short gator legs carrying it across the lobby. It was moving fast. Something was clamped between its powerful jaws, but I couldn't make out what it was.

So this is the rascal Ethel told me about.

The funeral dirge the gator was too short to have activated now rang out, and I turned my head back to the front.

A ways behind the gator but losing ground, Lurch put in a valiant effort at pursuit, his tree trunk legs taking enormous strides. Over his resort costume, a formal three-piece suit fitting for a funeral director, he wore a heavy down jacket that made him look like a thinner version of the Michelin tire man, a football helmet, and over one hand an ice hockey goalie glove. In his ungloved hand he carried...

What is that?

I squinted—a collapsed umbrella from one of the tables by the pool. *Huh.*

Odeo, the sturdy head grounds keeper, similarly outfitted, loped along behind Lurch. Both arms were rolled in heavy quilted moving pads that had been taped to stay in place. His weapon of choice was an enormous pair of hedge shears.

Behind Lurch and Odeo, two of Odeo's groundsmen followed, more slowly and with much less enthusiasm—one carrying a rake, the other a shovel.

"There they go again." Cat had stepped up beside me. "The Gator Brigade."

If it hadn't been for the gator who was now terrifying the guests in its attempts to find an escape route, it would have been hysterical. The gator ran one way, opened its jaws, and dropped what I could now see was a straw tote bag on the floor then hissed at the scattering tourists in its path. Then it scooped up the bag and scooted another way only to be met by the Gator Brigade who chased it back toward the front desk in an effort to get it out the door.

But the gator didn't seem to have checking out in mind, and when it neared the open double doors, it turned yet again, heading back into the lobby. At one point Lurch managed to corner it using the now open patio umbrella as both shield and rapier.

The gator refused to surrender and lunged at the umbrella, sending Lurch and his backup team of Odeo and the two groundsmen backpedaling like crazy. The gator raised itself up as tall as its T. rex legs could and made a beeline for the front desk, circling around behind it, sending the desk clerk, Lucy, leaping onto the top of the counter.

Everything went suddenly quiet as Lurch, Odeo, and the two quaking groundsmen did their level best to sneak up on it.

The Gator Brigade came to a head-scratching, dumbfounded stop, and Odeo asked, "Well, where'd she go? She can't just up and disappear like that? Can she?" He looked up at Lurch who lifted his impossibly broad shoulders in confusion and moaned. Odeo shook his head. "Ain't right no gator be acting like that. Something wrong with it. Maybe it's a haint."

"A haint?" Cat was skeptical.

I shrugged. "Nothing a little haint blue paint wouldn't cure. My Grandmamma Ida would surely know what to do." Grandmamma Ida knew all about how to keep spirits at bay. "You think maybe this gator really is the pirate Jean Lafitte who's come back to find his letter of pardon?"

Cat's turn to shrug. "Well, if it is possessed, I guess Jean Lafitte's as good a spirit to be possessed by as any of 'em."

"But the gator's gone now." I looked at her. "Where'd it go?"

She grinned, shook her head, and spread her fingers. "Poof."

"Seriously?"

"This is what's been happening. The gator shows up on the grounds out back of the resort or runs around inside, creates a bit of chaos, and disappears into thin air. But it always comes back."

"What was it doing with that tote bag?"

"Well, a pirate's a pirate, after all—gather a little treasure here and there. It's what pirates do."

"Right," I said. "If that gator's the reincarnation of Jean Lafitte, then I'm Marie Laveau."

She laughed and took me by the hand. "Well, come on then, Marie, and use one of your voodoo spells to rustle us up some lunch."

CHAPTER FOUR

———

After lunch, Cat went back to the House of Cards for her afternoon appointments, and I headed back over to Dragons and Deities Tattoo Parlor, where I had a couple of hours working on a teenage boy who'd asked for the elaborate Hogwarts crest on his right back shoulder and then a newlywed couple who'd asked for the other's astrological sign and birthdate to be tattooed over their hearts.

It was after three o'clock when I met Cat back at the Presto-Change-o Room for a glass of wine and catching up on my trip and her life.

She was appalled at the way Jack's mother had behaved toward me and about as miffed as I was that Jack hadn't seemed to set her straight. "If I'd have ever thought anyone wouldn't stand for the woman he loves to be cold-shouldered, it'd be your Cap'n Jack. Always figured that Yankee boy to be as hot-blooded and passionate as any Southern man."

I sipped the Roux St. Louis, one of my favorites from Pontchartrain Vineyards, and tried to sort out my feelings while Cat went on about how Jack *should* have handled it, which had a lot of remarks about setting the "old girl straight." Having Cat waxing indignant about things surely was a comfort, and I appreciated it. But I wasn't sure her unflagging loyalty was what I really needed at that point. I'd heard Jack's side of things from him, how he'd supposedly taken his mother aside and asked her to be kinder and more considerate of me. Whether he'd done it or not hadn't seemed to make a difference in the standoffish attitude Mrs. Stockton presented, and that had made me wonder if he'd actually spoken to her. But I'd mellowed since yesterday, and I'd already halfway forgiven him for what I thought of as being wimpy about it. Although the thoughts of an unbiased individual at that point would probably have helped me really see Jack's point of view.

As if reading my mind, Cat said, "You kind of have to look at it from behind Jack's eyes too, though. I mean, she's his mother and all—you know, a certain amount of respect's involved. And nobody knows her better than he does. Maybe she's the kind you can't hit over the head with something. Maybe all you can do is plant the seed of suggestion then stand back and let her water it and nurture it until it blooms on its own."

She sat there looking at me, waiting for a response, which I gave in the form of a hug after finishing off my wine. "Wise beyond your years, Gabor. Wise beyond your years. I'm going to find him, hug him, tell him I love him, and make sure he knows I understand."

But all those good intentions went straight down the toilet when I walked back into the lobby and saw Jack and Sydney coming through the front doors to the accompaniment of the funeral dirge. They were laughing and looking very chummy. She stepped around in front of him, and when he stopped walking, she threw her arms around his neck and kissed him square on the mouth.

I saw fifty shades of red, and without stopping to think about what I was doing, I marched over, took hold of her arm, and pulled her off him.

I couldn't say who was more startled, Jack or Sydney.

"It isn't how it looks, Mel," he said quickly, his face flush—from guilt, maybe?

"It better not be." I stood back, crossed my arms, and waited.

Sydney smirked and tossed her curly locks. "And how does it look?"

Instead of punching her in the face, which was what I wanted to do, I turned to Jack. "She needs to leave. You should tell her to leave. Now."

He looked upset, even confused (which I didn't understand). There was no response right away, but when it came, it couldn't have been worse. "I can't do that," he said, his voice so soft it was almost a whisper.

My movement backward was more stagger than step, as if I was the one who got punched in the face. "Can't? Or won't?"

"Mel." He reached for me, but I leaned away, out of his reach. "She's a paying guest."

My heart broke in two, but somehow I managed to bottle up the sob that rose from the deepest place in my soul. I wouldn't cry in front of Lurch and Lucy and the twenty or so guests in the lobby area, and I certainly wouldn't give either Jack or Sydney the satisfaction of crying in front of her.

I started to snap back at her, but my voice was gone, so I drew myself up to my full height—at least I was taller than the bitch—lifted my chin, and walked out.

I didn't even have to think twice about it. I had to leave Mystic Isle, at least for a while. I couldn't occupy the same space as Sydney Baxter. It would eventually wind up with assault charges being filed against me, and I felt Jack needed to handle this by himself. It wasn't up to me to hand out her orders to vacate the premises—and the man.

Marching straight out front, I flagged down one of Odeo's groundsmen on a golf cart—it was Ralph, one of the guys I'd seen on gator detail earlier. I breathed in and out a few times to let off some steam so as not to scare him away. "Y'at, Ralph? Got time to run me over to *la petite maison*?"

He was a lanky scarecrow of a guy with scraggly straw-colored hair sticking out from under a Pelicans cap. He smiled and nodded. "Sure thing, Miss Hamilton. Hop on."

La petite maison was at the end of a zigzag roadway a ways from the hotel building. Back in the 1700s, when the plantation had come to be, the smaller one-story red-brick version of the big house served as an office where the plantation owner went over his accounts and who knew what else. Now, centuries later, it had been elegantly remodeled into a Southern manor worthy of a gentleman like Harry Villars. He lived there with my gentle good friend and resort faux medium, Fabrizio Banini, affectionately known as the Great Fabrizio.

Ralph let me off in front of the house behind a big black limousine. Harry and Fabrizio stood by the rear of the limo as the driver unloaded luggage from the trunk.

Fabrizio came over to me as I stepped away from the golf cart. "Lovely timing, my dear." His British accent made him sound as wise and dignified as it always did, although there was a tinge of fatigue behind it. Fabrizio was fifty or so and probably not as spry as he'd once been. Striking and tall, still slender, with longish grey hair that he mostly wore pulled back in a low ponytail, Fabrizio was handsome in the distinguished way aging stage actors always seemed to be. He had a kind and tender heart he wore on his sleeve where it was easily bruised by even the slightest of bumps.

"I'm so sorry," I began. "You must be tired." I couldn't believe I'd forgotten Harry and Fabrizio had taken a week's sojourn to Key West at the same time Jack and I had made the fateful trip to Palm Beach. "I should give you two some time to get your feet under you before I come marching in."

He took hold of my hand. "Don't be silly, my dear. You're always welcome here. Harry feels the same way." He pulled me closer to the limo. "Don't you, Harry?"

"Don't I what?" Harry turned toward us, reaching out to clasp my free hand. "How are you, Miss Hamilton? So pleased to see you."

"And you," I said. "Did you enjoy Key West?"

He smiled and lolled his head to one side. "Why, yes, we did. Didn't we, Fabrizio? But it's surely so hectic there, running here, running there, trying to see all our friends and fulfill all our social obligations. It's just real nice to finally get home. And how was your trip with Mr. Stockton?"

I looked at my feet as emotion surged. Both Harry and Fabrizio picked up on how things were as if they were the real deal psychics Harry purported to employ at The Mansion.

"Oh no, my dear," Harry said.

"What happened?" Fabrizio trilled.

"I…I…" I didn't want to go into it, but knew I'd have to before I could state the reason for my visit.

"You come on in the house, dear, and let us fix you a lovely cup of chamomile tea," Harry said.

I shook my head.

"She should come in, shouldn't she, Fabrizio?" he coaxed.

"Of course she should."

"Ralph's waiting for me. He has work to do." I lifted the hand held by Fabrizio to indicate Ralph in the golf cart.

"Ralph, is it?" Harry began, and Ralph nodded. "You can wait here a while for Miss Hamilton. If there are any problems from Mr. Fournet about you shirking your duties as groundsman, you can refer him to me."

Ralph shrugged and nodded before shutting off the golf cart motor.

Harry and Fabrizio led me to the porch and up to the glossy red front door where we paused.

"I need to leave The Mansion," I said. "I have to get away from here—from things. If I clear my calendar, could I have a week off? Or even a few days? I just can't bear it." Oh my God, I thought, the Scarlett O'Hara is coming out in me. *Oh, Rhett, wherever shall I go? Whatever shall I do?*

But that was straight up in Harry's wheelhouse—Southern sympathy. His voice took on a soothing tone. "Come in, Miss Hamilton. You can tell us all about it once we're inside. This sounds as if it might be a matter of the heart, and those things are best discussed behind a closed door where there aren't any big ears to pick up on things."

I looked behind me to see Ralph rubbing his earlobes, a puzzled look on his face. I almost laughed. I did smile. Harry Villars nearly always had that effect on me.

He took his key from the pocket of his lime green rayon slacks and fit it into the keyhole. It turned freely, and he said, "Well, now that's peculiar. The door's open."

Fabrizio said, "That is rather strange, Harry. I distinctly remember having watched you lock it prior to our leaving."

Harry took hold of the handle and pressed down on the latch. He pushed, and the door swung open.

All three of us stepped back and covered our faces.

"*Mon Dieu!*" Harry exclaimed.

"Bloody hell!" Fabrizio choked.

I couldn't speak for a moment, struck dumb by the awful stench that assaulted us from inside the house. I waited in the foyer as Harry and Fabrizio went in, disappearing into this room then that one off the main hallway.

The odor was rotten, the most horrible thing I'd ever experienced. "God, I said. What is that?" Dirty socks? Rancid garbage? Whatever it was— "It smells like something curled up and died."

Harry stood framed in the open door at the end of the hallway, his back to me. His voice shook. "Not something. Some*one*."

CHAPTER FIVE

———

When Harry grabbed onto the doorjamb and sagged, I rushed in and took his arm, propping him up. With one shaking hand, he pointed me in the direction of his prized claw-foot tub. A man lay propped up against it. I'd watched enough *CSI* to know that the odd angle of the neck and the smear of blood behind the head indicated a violent death for this person—whoever he was.

"What's going..." Fabrizio walked up behind us and peered over my shoulder. "My word...who is that?"

"You don't know?" I asked.

Both men shook their heads. None of us could seem to look away from the awful sight of the poor man's mottled skin, gaping mouth, and claw-stiff fingers.

"The front door was open," I said. "This could be someone who broke into your house."

"I need to sit down," Harry said, turning away from the horrific sight.

I turned with him, noticing as I did that a towel bar had been pulled from the wall and that the voluminous shower curtain had been partially yanked off the overhead rod. The dead man still clutched one corner of it in his hand.

"Let's go outside and wait for the sheriff," I said. "We can't even breathe in here."

As we made our way down the hall, it was impossible not to notice the state of things in the house—open drawers with the contents spilling out, chair and sofa cushions pulled off onto the floor, artwork askew on the walls.

"That chap broke in here and went looking for something." Fabrizio stated the obvious. "What could it be?"

"I certainly don't know," Harry said. This was obviously hitting him hard. And why wouldn't it? Someone having died in his home? It would have hit *me* hard. "What do you think happened to that poor soul?"

Fabrizio said. "From what I saw, he came to a bit of a sticky end."

Every once in a while, the drama from Fabrizio's days on British stages caught up with him.

I gave him a knock-it-off look then said, "I'm calling Jack." And I did, telling Jack what had happened and that I was sending Ralph over in the cart to pick him up at the front entrance—all the while I was speaking to him, I wondered whether he was with Sydney Baxter.

Jealousy is an ugly toxic beast that was living and thriving in my heart just then. So when Jack hopped out of Ralph's golf cart and rushed to put his comforting arms around me, all I could do was stiffen up and avoid looking at him. Jack obviously felt my discomfort and didn't prolong the hug. "Are you up to showing it to me?" he asked, speaking to no one specifically.

Neither Harry nor Fabrizio would meet his eyes, making it obvious they didn't want to go back into the house. Looked like it was up to me.

"Follow me." I motioned Jack inside and went halfway up the hall, my hand covering my nose. I found I was unable to go all the way back to the bathroom and stopped dead in the middle of the hall. Jack went the rest of the way by himself, stopping just outside the doorway and leaning in, his back to me.

His shoulders sagged, and his head drooped.

Under his breath, he said, "I managed the Kramer Central Park for five years without a single dead body on my watch. What is it about this place?"

I had to wonder the same thing as I escaped back out to the front porch where Harry and Fabrizio sat side by side on a wooden porch swing. Their hands were clasped together, stress evident in their knitted brows and concerned eyes.

Chief Deputy Quincy Boudreaux, the movie star handsome and slightly mad in that wild-eyed Cajun way representative of Jefferson Parrish Sheriff's Department and my best friend's fiancé, arrived within ten minutes of Jack, chauffeured by Sergeant Pam Mackelroy, also of the sheriff's office.

By that time both Harry and Fabrizio had worked themselves into such a state they could hardly function, but between the four of us, we managed to field Quincy and Sergeant Mackelroy's questions.

Where had Harry and Fabrizio been the last week, as well as Jack and I, for that matter? *Florida. All of us, but not together.*

And when had we all arrived back at Mystic Isle? *Jack and I last night. Harry and Fabrizio just a couple of hours ago.*

Was anyone expected at *la petite maison*—serviceman, painter, cleaner? *No one except maid service, the usual resort staff, all female.*

And considering that the house had been tossed, what were they looking for? There was no answer to that one, none that we knew anyway.

The forensics team arrived maybe a half hour after Quincy, about the same time as Ralph made another delivery with the golf cart. This time it was Cat, who was done with her schedule for the day and had come to lend moral support. She stepped up onto the porch and took me in her arms. "Oh my goodness, girl. This is just getting to be too much. We need to ask the cosmos to give us here at Mystic Isle a break from all the dead bodies piling up lately."

I didn't know what time it was exactly, but the sun was setting, so I figured sixish. The pillar and landscape lighting switched on automatically. The air was definitely cooler. I shivered and rubbed my arms, and Jack, who'd read my mood and been smart enough to keep his distance until then, came up behind me and began to shrug out of his sport coat.

I held up a hand. "No thank you, Jack. You keep it. I'm fine."

"Mel, don't." His voice pleaded as hurt rose in his amber eyes, tightening his lips.

I hadn't meant to hurt him, but I obviously had. My heart squeezed. "Aw, Jack, let's get this all straightened out. Send Sydney home."

He looked over to where Harry and Fabrizio stood looking worried and upset. "I'm trying," Jack said softly then, "I will."

I didn't understand, but this wasn't the time or place to dig any deeper. I laid my hand on his arm before turning away.

Quincy and Pam Mackelroy came back out of the house with one of the forensics techs. His eyes warming when he caught sight of Cat, Quincy announced, "This appears to be an accidental death." He walked over to Harry and showed him a man's wallet, flipping it open to a photo ID. I couldn't see it from where I stood, but I thought it might have been a driver's license. "The man was Elroy Villars," Quincy said.

Harry's intake of breath was audible. "Villars? Sir, how's that possible?"

Quincy shrugged. "You're asking me?"

Harry just sat there blinking. "Chief Deputy, I never heard of someone in the Villars family named Elroy."

"Looks to me like he might be related, Mr. Villars," Quincy said, closing the wallet then dropping it into an evidence bag that Sergeant Mackelroy had opened for him. "I called it in, and there's already a BOLO out on him. He's been missing since Thursday. The family is being notified. It seems they're guests right here at Mystic Isle."

"Now we know why," Sergeant Mackelroy said.

"Time of death looks like maybe Thursday night. At first glance, the ME figures our victim in there got turned around and confused in the dark and hit his fool head on the tub. So it seems like he might have been having himself a look around *la petite maison*, you know, maybe see what he can find to carry off while his relative is out of town. Doesn't look like that was such a good plan for him now, does it?"

Sergeant Pam Mackelroy snorted unattractively. *Twit!* Cat and I both knew too well that Mackelroy carried an Olympic-sized torch for Quincy and not only laughed at practically everything he said, whether it was funny or not, but she also backed him a hundred percent, right or wrong. Consequently, Cat always kept a sharp eye on the good sergeant to make sure she kept things strictly professional with the dashing chief deputy.

At Mackelroy's snorting, Quincy's dark eyes skewed a quick glance in her direction before turning back to Harry. "I think we're gonna wait for the ME to make a final call on this, and I won't be running a homicide investigation right away. We're saying *accidental death* for now, but the house, she's still a crime scene until we know for sure."

Harry stood. "No problem, Chief Deputy. Our bags are still packed. We'll just catch us a ride back to the resort and take a room there, just 'til things settle down a might, mind you."

Fabrizio waved a hand in front of his nose. "And until someone comes to fumigate the place."

"The Presidential Suite is vacant for the time being," Jack said. "I'll have your bags taken over."

Because there were so many of us who needed to head back to the resort, Jack called for one of the shuttle buses to come and pick us all up.

Cat sat with me in the lavishly decorated shuttle with Jack just across the aisle. We pulled away from *la petite maison*, leaving the sheriff's office detail working to remove the poor man's body and document the scene.

Quincy looked up to watch us leave, his handsome features shaded by the hand shielding his eyes from the sun. Cat pressed her lips up against the window, leaving a red imprint. Quincy grinned and blew a kiss back then tapped his heart with one fist. Behind him Sergeant Mackelroy crossed her arms, looking grumpy.

"It must be so sad for her," I whispered in Cat's ear. "I mean that man's stone-cold gone for you, and little Pammie doesn't even stand half a chance."

"Mel." Jack's voice pulled my attention away, and I turned to look at him.

Cap'n Jack—it was how I'd thought of my devilishly handsome boss from day one. When he first came to Mystic Isle after weathering a disaster of biblical proportions in the Big Apple, namely having mistakenly bedded the sexy young wife of the hotel chain's CEO, I'd had such a crush on him I fell apart whenever he came around me. Imagine my extreme happiness when I'd discovered this tall, well-built man with eyes like warm brandy felt the same way about me. The mutual admiration society had turned into real affection and then, I could hardly believe it, love. Jack had even wanted to take me to meet his parents.

That was when the trouble began.

Wasn't he supposed to be my dashing buccaneer swinging from the yardarm to snatch me from the jaws of danger—and a spiteful mother? My Cap'n Jack. It made me sad that something had come between us, something as immovable as a mother—and I wasn't using that term figuratively.

The thought must have reflected on my face because he asked, "Are you okay?"

I nodded, just wanting everything to go back to the way things were before we went to Florida, before his mother hurt my feelings, before his old girlfriend came around trying to wiggle her way back into his heart.

"I'm fine." *Your nose is gonna grow, girl.* "I think I'm going to give you some space to deal with"—I tried to think of a way to express things without having to say her stupid name—"our problem. I'll be leaving the cottage. A few days anyway. You can keep me posted on how things are going."

He looked at me a long time. "I wish you wouldn't do this, but I understand. At least I think I do. I'm so sorry this is happening."

I just nodded my acknowledgement.

Cat had been facing the window, pretending not to hear us. Without looking away from the glass, she picked up my hand and held it.

It was suddenly really quiet on the shuttle, the only sound the growl of the motor.

We rode that way for a minute before Jack cleared his throat and began. "Did you hear what Quincy said about the dead man being Elroy Villars?" He didn't wait for me to answer. "Isn't that one of the names we heard on the plane, on that newscast?"

Cat turned from the window. "Elroy and Percy Villars." She joined the conversation. "The names of the twins who claim to be descended from Jean Lafitte and Belle Villars. They're a part of the treasure hunters looking for the document. In fact, the Villars twins are the main reason all those other folks are here. But the Villars twins had a leg up on the others. They have a journal from their ancestor that actually details the location of where the document was hidden on the plantation."

"Twins," Jack said slowly. "So the deceased has a brother."

Cat nodded. "Staying at the resort. There's a sister. I heard that she's here too."

"How do you know all this?" I asked, pretending to be so involved in the death that nothing else mattered. Not true.

"Because when his twin brother up and disappeared, Percy booked a reading with me. Told me all about everything." She shook her head. "I couldn't help him, of course. And now it doesn't look like anyone can help. He seemed like a nice enough guy, and I feel sorry for his loss. It's times like this I'd like to be a real fortune teller, not just one of Harry's cast members. Maybe there was something I could have done to prevent this."

I gave her a sympathetic look, understanding what she meant. But I had to acknowledge, at least to myself, there were times Cat was so intuitive I wondered if she wasn't the real deal after all.

When we arrived back at the front of the main resort building and got off the shuttle, who stood waiting on the veranda but that dang interloper, Sydney Baxter.

She ran up to Jack and took hold of his arms. "Oh, sweetheart, baby—"

I bristled and fisted my hands. *Sweetheart? Baby? He's my Cap'n Jack, bitch, back off.*

She went on, words oozing thick as molasses from her Strawberries 'n' Cream Pink glossed lips. "I missed you while you were gone." She cast me a shrewd—no, not shrewd—evil glance. "What delicious thing do you have planned for us tonight?"

"Is that her?" Cat whispered.

"Oh, yes," I whispered back, well, more a hiss really.

"She looks like Shirley Temple, f'sure," Cat said softly. "You don't have anything to worry 'bout, *ma chère souer*. You are everything, and she…she's…"—a pause as she seemed to be thinking—"she's blonde."

Jack removed Sydney's hands from him and stood back from her. "I'm not available to entertain you tonight, Syd. You're on your own. But there's plenty here at the resort to keep you occupied." It looked to me like he actually did try to walk away from her, or maybe that was just wishful thinking on my part. Whatever Jack intended, Sydney seemed unfazed and ran inside after him, latching right back onto him like some creepy old swamp leech or something.

CHAPTER SIX

———

I didn't have any appointments for the rest of the day, so I went up the grand winding staircase with Harry and Fabrizio to see if they needed any help settling in and if not, then just for moral support.

The Presidential Suite, while like nothing so grand as might be found in a larger hotel, was still lovely. It consisted of a large parlor, dining area with a tiny bar and staging kitchen, and a separate bathroom. The balcony of the large and graceful bedroom looked out over the resort's front lawn area and beyond to the murky, mossy waters of the lazy and lovely Louisiana bayou where the Spanish moss cascaded from live oak trees like waterfalls and the knees of the cypress trees bulged at the waterline.

I opened the French doors, walked out there, and watched as a couple of cranes maneuvered the lily pads on the surface of the pond. Fabrizio came up beside me.

"The raw beauty of this place never fails to impress me," he said. "When I lived in England and thought of swampland, it was never quite as amazing as this."

"Mmm."

He was right. It was magnificent in a unique way.

"Melanie," he began tentatively, and I figured he was about to ask something of me, so I turned from the incredible view to face him. "Harry's upset about the body in the bathroom."

No great revelation there. "Perfectly understandable," I said. "I'm upset about it, and it isn't even my bathroom."

"It would mean a lot to him if you would by chance consider postponing your leave of absence until things have quieted down a bit. I hate to ask."

I didn't answer right away but turned around and looked inside the suite's bedroom room where Harry was unpacking one of their suitcases. His slumped and defeated posture bespoke his disheartened feelings without words. As Harry moved between the suitcase on the bed and the bureau, he shook his head, sighing. When he turned back around, the unhappiness in his eyes, the worry and stress etched on his face tugged at my heart. This sad and worried man wasn't the joyful, free-spirited Harry I'd come to know. It was a rare occasion to see this man without a smile. He'd removed the jacket from his three-piece suit and had hung it on the clothes tree. His signature Panama hat topped the tree, making it look like a headless man.

Harry Villars was a throwback to a different time. His manners were flawless. His style, impeccable. His character, unimpeachable. As an employee of the resort, I hadn't known him all that well until I came to see his goodness through the loving eyes of my friend, Fabrizio, Harry's significant other.

Fabrizio and I had shared a bond from the day he came to The Mansion at Mystic Isle and had been hired to portray the resort's medium. Fabrizio reminded me so much of my Granddaddy Joe, the strong male presence in my life when I was growing up. I missed my Granddaddy Joe every day. He'd "moved on," as he'd put it, when I was eighteen, and a day never went by without my thinking about him. He'd promised to always be with me, and there were definitely times I knew he was. His voice would come to me at times when I needed advice or help, and I always listened. I'd have been a fool not to.

But my Granddaddy Joe was also with me in Fabrizio—well, sort of. He was there in Fabrizio's laugh, his gentle smile, his love of art and music (and in Fabrizio's case, the dramatic arts). My granddaddy was there in the way Fabrizio was so, so present when listening to something that bothered me or something that pleased me. My Granddaddy Joe was the reason I'd bonded with Fabrizio to begin with, but the gentleness and generous spirit of the British actor were what kept us that way.

Because Harry made Fabrizio happy, he loomed large in my heart as well.

"Why does Harry want me to postpone taking some time away from the resort?" I asked.

"Well, m'dear, sweet Harry is nothing if not a superstitious sort, and since you were instrumental in calming things down and clearing things up when we've had trouble in the past"—I assumed trouble in the past referred to two recent murders that happened on resort property—"he's come to think of you as somewhat of a good luck charm, if you will."

Good luck charm, eh?

Right.

And besides, if Harry Villars thought it was bad juju for me to leave, then the least I could do for the man who signed my generous paycheck, and those of my lover and my friends, was to stick around and see him through this.

But I had to wonder why this was hitting him so much harder than other deaths that had occurred on the premises—not that those had him jumping for joy or anything, but he hadn't seemed nearly so devastated by them.

As if reading my mind, Fabrizio began, "That young man who died, Elroy Villars?"

I turned back to Fabrizio, and he went on. "He and his brother have said they're descendants of Belle Villars, a biracial slave from this very plantation back in the early 1800s. While they may not be blood relatives, Harry's considering them family of sorts. He's taking this whole thing straight into his heart, and it's already weighing him down."

I looked back at Harry, who was moving even more slowly than before.

"I can see that," I said to Fabrizio then walked back inside and went straight to the bed, taking a few immaculately folded and pressed shirts from it and carrying them to the bureau where Harry was putting a few other items in a drawer. "Let me help," I said.

Harry turned and took them from me. "I'm so sorry about what happened, Harry," I said. "Do you believe it's true that man is related to someone from the plantation?"

He shrugged, taking a moment to smooth his already impeccable mustache even more. "I'm not sure yet, but you know how I am, Miss Hamilton. I tend to rely on my intuition. It hasn't steered me wrong so far, and right now, it's telling me that young man was a Villars. Now what he thought he was doing in my abode in the middle of the night whilst I was absent is another thing. Nevertheless, I can't help but feel badly about his demise." He hung his head.

I laid my hand on his arm. "Of course," I said. "I have a proposition for you. As I told you earlier before we…well, before, I've been staying with Jack Stockton in his cottage on the premises—"

"I know," he said. "I'm a longtime aficionado of romance, Miss Hamilton. I have no objection to your staying there with him. Fabrizio has pled your case with gusto, and if anyone understands the ways of true love, it is I."

"Well, you see, I need to put some space between Jack and me right now, but at the same time, I want to be here for you if it makes you feel better during this ugly time. Quincy is staying with Cat at our apartment while they're planning their wedding, and honestly, I'd feel like a third wheel staying there, so, I was wondering if…" I let my voice trail off.

"Say no more, Miss Hamilton. We'll find you a place to sojourn in private right here at the resort while you're reconciling with Mr. Stockton. And if time away from your studio would help you to sort through your feelings, I have no problem if you'd prefer keeping your work schedule light."

Fabrizio walked up beside Harry and put his arm around Harry's shoulders.

"Would that suit you?" Harry asked.

I stretched out my arms toward Harry, presenting the folded shirts. "You, Mr. Villars, are what my Grandmamma Ida says is a rare find these days, a true Southern gentleman. Thank you for your kind consideration."

"Oh no, Miss Hamilton." Harry lifted the shirts and laid them in the open bureau drawer. "Thank *you* for your kind consideration. I truly believe the cosmos appreciates your presence here at Mystic Isle."

CHAPTER SEVEN

While Lucy, the front desk clerk on duty, was assigned the chore of finding a room that would be vacant for the next week at least, I sat and waited with Fabrizio in the suite's parlor. Harry called Percy Villars' room and made arrangements to meet with him in the main salon.

Fabrizio begged off. "This all has me completely knackered, just wanting a bath then a pillow."

Harry admitted, "I have to say I'm a little on the nervous side 'bout meeting up with this young man, although he did seem nice enough on the phone. Sad, yes, but pleasant. Still, not knowing what to expect and all, I'd certainly consider it a lagniappe if you'd come along when I meet with him, Miss Hamilton. You have such a sweet way of dealing with folks."

A lagniappe? A favor? It was hard not to think that Harry was playing the boss card. Although I didn't usually think of him that way, the bad experience I'd had in Florida, followed with this Sydney person showing up here, had me just the slightest bit cynical. I made a conscious effort to thrust those feelings aside.

"Sure," I said.

It might have been the Pollyanna coming out in me, but I truly did think Harry's gentle soul wouldn't—no, couldn't—allow him to coerce me to help him.

And besides, Lucy hadn't found me a room yet, so I didn't have anywhere else to go anyway.

After another twenty minutes or so of Harry nervously fussing about while laying out his toiletries in the bathroom then calling downstairs for extra pillows and blankets, he finally glanced at the time. "Well, I suppose we oughta head on down, if you're still of a mind to," he said to me while shrugging on the pastel blue jacket he'd had on earlier when they arrived from the airport. It was a strange color to have picked to coordinate with the lime green slacks, but oddly enough, it worked.

We headed downstairs and crossed the lobby to the main salon, which was at the front of the building just to the right as you came in through the entrance. It was an enormous room, high-ceilinged, longer than wide. Floral-patterned oval rugs set off conversation areas where antebellum-style settees had been placed. The far end of the room was occupied by small café-style tables where wine, cocktails, and hors d'oeuvres were served during happy hour.

Tatiana was at the keyboard of the ivory baby grand, "Sentimental Journey" rolling softly from under her fingertips. She was a lovely elderly woman Harry had recently hired to play her special brand of soothing music four nights a week during happy hour. An elegant dame, Tatiana always showed up for work coiffed like she'd come straight from the beauty salon and wearing an evening gown. She nodded at Harry and winked with a bit of a come-hither look. She obviously didn't realize she wasn't anywhere close to Harry's type or that he'd been taken completely off the market anyway when he and Fabrizio had become a couple.

At one of the far tables, a man stood and waved. "That must be Percy," I said.

"Must be." Harry nodded and waved back, but his tone was quiet and uncertain.

We headed on back to the table where a woman sat, while the man continued standing. He offered his hand to Harry. "Percy Villars." His demeanor was subdued, and his eyes were swollen and red-rimmed, reminding me that he'd probably just learned his brother had been killed. I appraised him in the dim light. There was no sign in Percy of the biracial slave the twins had claimed to have been descended from.

He was average height and build, somewhat ginger, with a fair, freckled complexion and hair a cross between red and light brown. It was his ears that made the biggest impression, and not in a good way. They were not only enormous but stuck almost straight out like somebody had opened both doors out wide on a Mack truck. His face was roundish, his mouth wide and full. His smile revealed a good-sized gap between his two front teeth. All in all, I couldn't shake the goofy image of Alfred E. Neuman from my mind and was horrified when I actually formed a mental picture of Percy on the cover of *Mad* magazine.

I tried to focus on his kind blue eyes as he gestured toward the blonde seated at the table. "Our—my sister, Nancy," Percy said.

Nancy shook hands, first with Harry then with me. "How do you do?" she said quietly. She was considerably taller and sturdier than her brother and looked nothing like him. Long, straight blonde hair had been parted on the side, swept across her brow then tucked behind her ears. Her face was nice but unremarkable with even features and blue eyes so pale that in the dim light of the main salon, they looked grey.

"All of us here at The Mansion are so terribly sorry for your loss," Harry said.

"Thanks." Percy looked down at his feet while Nancy took a tissue from her purse and blew her nose—loudly.

"Should we sit?" Harry asked.

"Oh, yeah, right," Percy said. "Sorry, I'm just—"

"Understandable," I said, sitting in the chair Harry was holding for me.

It took a long minute for any of us to say anything further, then Harry broke the ice. "I understand you two and your brother came here hoping to locate an historical document you believe to be hidden here."

Percy and Nancy both nodded. It was Percy who spoke first. "You've heard the story of our ancestor, Belle Villars, haven't you, Harry? May I call you Harry?"

"Of course."

"Traces of her have almost all but been removed from our line, but she kept the family name of her masters. It was the only name she knew, and she raised her son as a Villars. That's how the name, our name, your name came to be handed down through the descendants of Belle and the pirate."

"I understand," Harry said, "and I want to welcome you to your ancestral home."

"Well, thank you," Percy said.

"This may not be the proper time to bring the subject up," Harry said hesitantly, "but I have to wonder what your brother—Elroy, is it?—might have been doing in my home whilst me and my partner weren't present."

Percy had the grace to hang his head. "I'm so sorry, Harry. I had no knowledge of Elroy's plan to break into your home. It isn't the proper way at all. I can't even imagine what he was thinking. When we arrived and learned you were out of town, we'd agreed the right thing to do was wait until you'd returned home to begin our quest." His face creased, and I thought he might start crying. "I don't understand…"

Nancy laid a hand on his arm. Although her eyes were moist, she was holding it together better than Percy. "Our brother didn't tell us. Neither of us knew in advance what he had planned, and we can only apologize for his behavior."

Percy shook his head. "Breaking in like a common burglar. What was he thinking?" He squeezed his eyes together, making his cheeks even more puffy. "If he'd told me, I'd have stopped him, and this never would have happened. He'd be here right now, talking with you, Harry, and you, Miss…"

"Melanie," I finished for him.

Percy stood suddenly, his gaze locked. "What have you learned, Deputy?"

Harry and I turned around to see who he was talking to.

Quincy Boudreaux came striding up to the table. Perky little Sergeant Mackelroy was missing in action this time. "Mel, Harry," Quincy said. "Mr. Villars, Miss Villars."

"What is it?" Percy asked.

"Do you recognize this?" Quincy laid a clear plastic evidence bag on the table in front of Percy, who sat down and stared at the contents—a yellowed and ripped notebook-sized sheet of paper with small, tight writing in thick black letters.

Percy looked at it a few beats then raised his head. "That's a page from Belle's journal," he said. "The page that specifies where she hid the letter of pardon she stole from Jean Lafitte." He looked at Quincy. "How did you come by this?"

"One of our deputies came across it caught up in one of the hibiscus bushes in the flower bed out front of your place, Harry. It looks like something torn from that journal your brother had?" He addressed his question to Percy. "Why would your brother have ripped it out like that?"

Percy stared at the evidence bag some more.

It was the sister who answered. "He wouldn't have. That journal is sacred text to my brothers. The two of them have huddled over it, studied it, memorized it, and treasured it for years and years. It's the key to the book deal they have."

"Book deal?" It was Quincy.

Percy lifted his gaze from the page inside the evidence bag. "My brother and I planned to write the story of Belle Villars and Jean Lafitte. We have—or had—a tentative deal with a New York publisher. The advance was contingent on our locating Lafitte's letter of pardon, the location of which was outlined in the journal. The publisher's rep was ecstatic about our book proposal, believed we'd have an international bestseller, a real blockbuster with movie rights in the millions. Finding that letter would lend legitimacy to our tale. It's why Elroy and I came down here."

I noticed Nancy squirming around in her chair and couldn't help wondering if locating the letter of pardon had been why the twins had traveled to Mystic Isle, what had brought Nancy here. "Are you involved in the book deal too?"

"Me?" Nancy pointed back at herself. "No."

Quincy was frowning, in full investigation mode now. I could always tell—his Cajun talk all but vanished. "What do you think this means? If that journal was so precious to you two, why would Elroy tear out this page, deface the journal? And if he knew from the journal where the letter was hiding, why would he tear the house apart like he did? This is getting kind of mysterious. Yes?"

I thought so too.

"Elroy made a mistake going to Harry's house and breaking in. That much is obvious." Percy leaned back in his chair, regarding us through his beady little eyes. He'd been running his hand through his curly red hair. It was standing straight up and his ears straight out. It was hard to take him seriously. "But he would never deface Belle's journal."

I had to ask. "If your brother knew where Belle hid the letter back then, why would he go all over and mess the house up like he did?"

Percy blinked his eyes rapidly, took a deep breath, and let it out. "He wouldn't. I've been so overwhelmed by Elroy's death I hadn't even stopped to think about all this, but not only would he not have torn the page out, he wouldn't even have broken in, much less have gone inside. He wouldn't have had to. Belle Villars hid the letter under the front porch of the building she described as Master Villars' accounting office."

Harry's expression was thoughtful. "The old accounting office? Under the porch?"

Percy nodded.

"That would be my porch, under the porch at *la petite maison.*"

Once again, Percy nodded.

"Do you think it's there?" Harry asked, looking at Percy.

It was Quincy who answered. "Well, folks, there is one way to find out." He picked up the evidence bag from the table. "Let's go."

CHAPTER EIGHT

———

I hadn't figured my going with Quincy and Harry and the other two back to *la petite maison* would wind up contributing anything, so I pulled Harry aside to speak with him.

"No reason I can see for me to go with you. If Elroy's death was an accident like Quincy thinks, there's nothing more to be learned by going back there. It's just Quincy scratching an itch."

Harry rubbed his chin. "Hmm. Scratching an itch? What does the good Chief Deputy Boudreaux hope to gain by crawling around under the porch of my house?"

I knew that one. "Because the good Chief Deputy Boudreaux can't stand a mystery of any kind, Mr. Villars. That man's gotta know everything about everything all the time. Bona fide control freak, that one. I don't know how Cat stands it, except she's got the knack of handling him down to a science. That's the reason their relationship works at all."

"Well, I do wish you'd come on along with us, Miss Hamilton. Your lovely presence makes any event festive and is a plus no matter what the occasion, even if it's just a bunch of deputies crawling around under my abode."

I sighed. What was it about me that Harry Villars had grown so attached to? I thought about begging off, but if I was honest with myself, I was every bit as curious about the death of Percy's brother and this Jean Lafitte mystery as Quincy was.

Even though I was born and bred in New Orleans, if I lived a hundred years, I'd never understand how word always spread so fast around here. By the time the four of us had ridden over to *la petite maison* with Quincy, there was already a good-sized crowd of people milling around outside the crime scene, which had been set apart with that yucky yellow crime scene tape.

I recognized some of the people—the Powells (Mr. and Mrs. Indiana Jones), some of the resort employees, Lurch, Odeo, as well as the other two members of the Gator Brigade who still wore their gator hunting outfits.

Jack was there and—*dammit*—Sydney, looking too cute for my comfort. I was at least gratified to see that Jack kept pushing her hands off his arm, then his chest, his shoulder, the back of his neck. He finally moved a couple of steps, managing to put Lurch between them. She was so touchy-feely I wouldn't have been surprised to see her manhandle Lurch again like she had in the lobby.

A second SUV from the Jefferson Parrish Sheriff's Office rolled up. It was good and dark by then in spite of the ground lighting Harry had so lovingly installed around his place, and a couple of deputies I hadn't seen before climbed out and got busy setting up pole lights around an area at one side of the house near the back.

Archie Powell, knobby knees sticking out from under a safari outfit similar to the one he'd had on during the interview, came right up to where we stood with Quincy. Powell was with another man—not tall, maybe five eight or so and compact, with a scruffy beard and dark, longish hair. This newcomer wore pale yellow slacks under a white long-sleeved dress shirt open down to the third button. The cuffs were folded up over the sleeves of a pastel blue jacket that had been pushed up on his forearms.

A third man stood just behind Powell. He wore headphones and was holding a shotgun-style mic on a boom that had been thrust in our general direction. A fourth guy stood beside him, his face jammed against the eyepiece on a camera attached to a complex system that looked to be part vest, part shoulder support.

Archie Powell spoke to Quincy. "Deputy?"

Quincy turned. "It's *Chief* Deputy Boudreaux." Quincy was really proud of his recent hard-won promotion.

Powell went on, offering his hand to Quincy. "I'm Archie Powell. This is Roger Goodwin." He indicated the guy channeling Sonny Crockett from *Miami Vice*. "Roger and his crew"—he jerked his head, and Quincy, Harry, and I turned to see two more guys standing back away from the rest of the crowd—"are documenting our search for the missing letter of pardon. Roger here is famous, you know."

"Oh really?" Quincy arched an eyebrow. "Famous for what?"

"Why Roger's a director, Deputy—"

"Chief Deputy."

"*Pharaoh's Ghost*." Powell folded his arms smugly across his chest. "You saw that, right?"

Quincy shook his head. "Don't think I know 'bout that one."

I knew who Roger Goodwin was, or at least who he had been, a well-thought-of movie director. After *Pharaoh's Ghost* had lost upwards of a hundred million dollars over its production costs, he'd pretty much disappeared from the public eye.

"I saw it," I said, wrinkling my nose. It had been a real stinker.

Roger turned to me then, white teeth flashing in his bearded face. "My biggest film yet. Huge budget. You know. Lots of CGI. That stands for computer graphic imagery."

"Actually," Harry interjected, "I do believe that's computer-*generated* imagery." He glanced around the group, smiling.

Theresa Powell, looking more like Lara Croft than ever, stepped into what I figured was the camera frame and laid a slender hand on Quincy's arm. Unfazed, Quincy moved his arm so that her hand fell away. Theresa Powell might be built like a brick house, but she didn't even begin to compare to the luscious Catalina Gabor.

"Chief Deputy," Theresa Powell said. "Roger is Mr. Hollywood himself."

The deputies switched on the lights they'd set up, which was when I noticed Roger's cream-colored canvas peasant shoes. No socks. Theresa was right as rain. Definitely Mr. Hollywood.

Roger Goodwin's question, by the turn of his head, included both Harry and Quincy. "So, what's going on out here? Word is you've found some indication of where the document might have been hidden."

Quincy didn't answer right away, which allowed time for Percy Villars to step up. "Listen, Powells. You need to back off with this search and this"—he gave the camera a disgusted look—"film you're making. That letter is mine and my brother's." He stopped cold a few long beats before correcting himself. "Well, now it's just mine." The head of steam he'd been building up seemed to have gone cold. He hung his head.

Archie Powell gave him a sympathetic look. "We heard about your family's tragedy. Our condolences for your loss. But, Percy, that document is going to belong to whomever puts their hand on it first. If it's you, then more power to you, but if we come across it before you do, then it's ours."

Roger drew everyone's attention when he said, "I trust you people have no objection to our filming whatever it is you're planning to do here?"

Quincy looked at Harry, who shrugged. Then Quincy shrugged too and said, "If it doesn't bother Harry, it doesn't bother me, long as you stay out of the way."

Roger scrubbed his hands together. "Terrific." He turned to the Powells. "After we get some footage of the sheriff's deputies doing their thing, we'll shoot your and Theresa's reactions."

Two of the deputies had been working at a hinged opening in the brick stem wall around the crawlspace under *la petite maison*. It wasn't very big. Not very big at all. If the letter was hidden somewhere under the porch, it wasn't going to be easy to get to.

Roger and the Powells, as well as dozens of others who'd gathered by now, watched as the same two deputies propped open that small hinged door and shone their searchlights into the dark space beyond it.

Roger asked, "And just what is it you'll be doing here, anyway?"

Quincy took a minute to study the opening and have a look around at the people nearby. His eyes finally settled on me. He laid his hand on my shoulder and grinned. "Why, Mr. Hollywood director, we're gonna have a look-see underneath this house. For buried treasure, don't you know? And this is the little gal we're sending on the hunt."

I looked around at him. Surely I hadn't heard him right. "Me?"

Quincy nodded. Harry looked surprised. The Powells and the Hollywood director turned to me with interested expressions.

"No," I said. "I won't go under there." My Grandmamma Ida had all kinds of bad things to say about what might lurk in the dark spaces under a house. Haints and monsters and beasties and all kinds of ugly things. And I, for one, had no desire to meet up with any of them. Harry's house had sat on that spot for well over two hundred years. That was plenty of time for any variety of evil, nasty things to take up residence under there.

I cast a worried glance in that general direction. "Nope. Huh-uh. No way."

"*Chère*," Quincy cajoled, his Cajun coming to the forefront. "It gotta be you, girl. Nobody else goin' fit that tiny hole."

He was wrong if he thought I'd succumb to that bayou charm. I shook my head but made the mistake of casting a look around. Harry, Percy, and Nancy Villars were all looking at me with what I could only call hope on their faces.

Harry's brows lifted in supplication.

"Really?" I said.

He shrugged and nodded. "I don't feel like there's any danger to you, Miss Hamilton. It would mean a lot to us to see what's under there. But of course you're free to choose for yourself."

I looked down at my resort costume, a black gown with a high collar around the back. I indicated the flowing skirt with my hands. "But I'm not dressed for—"

"No worries," Quincy said. "Deputy Washington there can go in the back of my car and get you a jumpsuit."

Of course he'd come prepared. The Jefferson Parrish Sheriff's Office and the Boy Scouts. Interchangeable.

I turned and stared at the hole in the stem wall and thought for sure I heard a voice, a voice that didn't speak to me but laughed—one of those long, low, evil laughs I'd heard in Scooby-Doo cartoons just before the monster jumped out at Scooby and Shaggy.

Bwa-ha-ha-ha-ha.

CHAPTER NINE

The air seemed suddenly colder, and I had the urge to hightail it out of there. Yep, I was scared, and I wasn't too big to admit it.

"Q, you know how I am about dark places." I tried to appeal to his kinder, gentler side.

Q, his chosen nickname by those few of us who knew and loved him well enough to overlook his brutal frankness (that he preferred to call a propensity to be candid), was a good-looking man. No doubt about it. But his hair didn't seem to know how to lie flat, always sticking up all over his head, and the reckless gleam in his eyes could have easily been mistaken for wickedness. Those traits were part of what made him innately sexy and a little intimidating. Good thing Cat had him on a silken leash. Together they were the most striking couple in the sixty-four parishes.

"Aw, come on, *chère*. Ain't nothing under there 'cept a few frogs and cucarachas. No boogie men." Okay, so Quincy didn't have a kinder, gentler nature.

"Q, please don't ask me to—" I took a quick look around the crowd, hoping to find an ally. Neither Cat nor Fabrizio was anywhere to be seen. And the only beloved face my gaze fell on was that of Jack Stockton. Cap'n Jack. *My* Cap'n Jack, who was at the moment staring at me with concern on his face. His eyes locked with mine but only for a brief moment. *Jack, I don't want to—*

My knight in shining armor suddenly looked down as the blonde threw herself against him, wrapped her arms around him, and looked up into his face. Her mouth was moving, but I was too far away to hear what she said. I could only see, and what I saw was my man staring down into her big stupid blue eyes.

As Fabrizio would have said if he were there, my ire was up.

Fine, Jack. I'll give you something to look at.

Quincy's deputy had come back from Quincy's SUV. In his hands he held a folded khaki-colored garment with a pair of like-colored gloves on top of it. I snatched them out of his hands.

"Haute couture, eh? Can I go inside the house to put this thing on?" I asked.

Quincy nodded at Deputy Washington, who led me around to the front of the house, took loose a strip of the tape, and stood back.

I went inside to a spot in the parlor where I didn't think anyone could see me through the windows, switched on a light, and changed into the jumpsuit. The horrific odor had mostly faded, but I could still smell it, or at least I imagined I could. When I finished zipping up the suit, I turned and checked out my reflection in one of the dark windows. *Swell, the ugly thing has all the charm and sex appeal of an old gunnysack.*

Yeah, right, Mel. Didn't think this through all that well, did you? How do you think you're gonna show up Jack's petite little ex looking like a sewer worker?

I stepped back outside. Deputy Washington was still there. Quincy probably told him to wait in case I made a break for it. Dang that Quincy Boudreaux. If he wasn't Cat's sweetie, I'd tell him exactly where to get off. I might anyway.

I walked back around to where everyone was still gathered. Waiting. For me?

I gulped when my gaze landed on the colorful soul who ran the resort's voodoo shop, Mambo Bon Magie. The voodoo "priestess," as she liked to be called, stood at the edge of the crowd. Mambo was a short, stout Creole with beautiful shiny black skin. The glare from lights the deputies had set up glinted off the enormous amber stone in her yellow turban with big purple polka dots. Her hands were folded over her round belly, and she was staring straight at me.

Almost as if she'd called my name, I felt the urge to go to her. So I did, stopping to stand right in front of her. She slipped a bead bracelet off her plump wrist and onto mine, mumbling some words I didn't understand as she did.

"You take this, child. Loa Eshu goin' protect you 'neath there."

I stared at her. "Under the house? There's something under the house I need to be protected from?"

She didn't answer.

"What? What is it I need protection from?"

She just patted my hand and smiled serenely.

I gulped and turned around to where Quincy, Harry, Percy, and Nancy Villars stood near the house by what I'd decided to call "the hellhole." Feeling like a condemned killer taking that last walk to sit and sizzle in old Gruesome Gertie, I pulled myself all the way up to my full five foot three inches, thrust my shoulders back, and went over to it.

The hinged opening in the stone stem wall wasn't very big at all, which was why I guessed Quincy had singled me out to be the one to take it on. I got down on my knees.

Quincy held out a small high-intensity penlight to me.

"You need to see where you gonna be going," he said. "Now in the page from the notebook, Belle says she hid the whale-skin pouch containing the document holder and Lafitte's important paper under what's now the porch in a hidey-hole where the second beam crosses the center. Understand?"

I nodded, took the light from him, and got down in the lush damp grass surrounding *la petite maison*, stretching out full length toward the dreaded gaping hole.

"You got this one, *chère*," Quincy said, giving me a thumbs-up.

I felt the presence of someone else behind me and twisted my head around.

The boom mic dropped into my field of vision, and I found myself staring into the eye of the movie camera.

Looking back up at Quincy, I said, "Really? You're going to let them film this fiasco? From behind?" I thought about what my rear end would look like in the stupid jumpsuit.

Roger Goodwin, aka Mr. Hollywood, rushed over and hunched down beside me. "Miss…? Sorry, I didn't get your name."

"My name doesn't matter," I said, suddenly anxious to get this show on the road and be done with it before I lost what little nerve I did have. My grandmamma and my mama would scold me for being impolite, but there it was. I'd also hear about it from them if they ever got wind of this stunt.

The director went on. "I just wanted to let you know that if we use the footage of you retrieving the letter of pardon from under the house, you'll be credited." He beamed at me. "What do you think of that? Eh?"

"Good to know." I narrowed my eyes and glared at Quincy then faced ahead into the opening, trying to ignore the dank, rotting smell drifting from it. It was dark under there—darker than dark. I quivered. "If the camera guy's going in with me anyway, why don't you just send him after the letter?"

It was Mr. Hollywood who answered. "Miss, surely you can see he won't fit all the way in. He'll go as far as possible, but that isn't a very big opening."

I sighed. He was right. The camera dude's shoulders would probably not even make it through.

Okay. "Well, here goes," I said to no one in particular as I clamped the penlight between my teeth, dug in with my elbows, and scooted myself, extended arms first, into the opening.

Behind me a cheer went up from the crowd. *Huh. Take that Sydney Baxter.* But that smugness evaporated when I looked ahead into the darkness. The cheers and applause quieted, and I was at the point of no return.

Twisting and turning, pushing, huffing and puffing, even grunting a little, I wedged myself in and finally through the opening. I was alone under a building that, across more than two centuries, had known life and death, pain and turmoil, cruelty and kindness, war and peace. Suddenly overwhelmed, my stomach and throat tightened with emotion, and I nearly gave in to the tears. Nearly but not quite.

Once I'd squeezed all the way in, the space opened up, and I could raise myself a little higher, which made movement a lot easier. I crawled forward ten feet or so.

Dampness soaked through the jumpsuit, giving me the shivers. It was quiet under there and as dark and tomb like as

Hades must have been once the dead crossed the river Styx. What little light I did have suddenly closed off, and I felt utterly alone. I looked back.

Okay, so I was as contrary as Mistress Mary, but at that point I welcomed the sight of Goodwin's cameraman with just one shoulder and elbow squeezed through the opening. He switched on a lamp and began to film me from behind. Jumpsuited backside and all.

But I didn't care anymore. Just knowing he was there and would be able to tell the world of my supreme sacrifice if a haint or the rougarou jumped me made me feel a tiny bit better. He switched on the camera and a light, and suddenly I could see, sort of.

The camera's light cast a hazy glow around and beyond me a ways, but as I moved farther under the roughhewn support beams and over the soft earth that had been reinforced here and there with small patches of uneven concrete, it grew suddenly darker. And I felt as if I were the last person alive on earth. Looking behind me, it was obvious the cameraman had withdrawn.

I made a noise in my throat that sounded a lot of like a whine, stopped crawling, took the penlight from between my teeth, and turned it on then put it back.

Off to my right something scuttled, and when I jerked at the sound, I bumped my head.

"Ow!"

As the penlight dropped to the ground, so did I, and my face nearly collided with the squishy earth.

I shuddered as something several inches long with pokey, prickly feet stalked across my fingers. The beam of the penlight caught it. Roach. Really, really big roach. I jerked, sending it flying.

Keep on a'goin'. It was a male voice in my head. A voice I recognized. Whenever I heard it or fancied I heard it, I always thought of it as my Granddaddy Joe who'd taught me most of what I know, if I could claim to know anything at all. Crawling around under a house with all things that slithered made me wonder if I did know anything. But there was the voice again. *You're doing jes' fine.*

I could see what I figured was the spot up ahead—few feet in from the front of the stone stem wall and just about dead center side to side, right where two heavy beams met.

I scooted along a little faster to get to it.

The dark. The closeness. The odor. It was getting to me pretty good. And then there was that sound. It sounded like an irritated baby. *Uh-uh-uh.* The sound went lower. *Oh-oh-oh.* I'd never heard a rougarou, so the sounds stopped me dead. I turned my head this way and that, hoping to God the beam of light didn't land on the vicious, gruesome, God-awful ugly hairy beast. It did land on a hairy beast, but it only turned out to be a big, old, fat swamp rat coming to see the fool human crawling around its domain. It sat there, its beady little eyes red and devil-like in the harsh beam of my little light.

"Get!" My hand settled on a small rock, which I chucked, and the thing scurried away—well, sort of. It was a bit too roly-poly of a swamp rat to do too much scurrying.

"You okay in dere, *chère?*" It was Quincy.

I didn't answer but aimed the penlight at my destination, now only a few feet in front of me, and continued my slow progress.

"*Chère?*" Louder this time.

"Get lost!" I yelled back.

I heard him tell someone. "She okay. Don't worry none."

And then I was there, the place where the beams met, the place where Quincy had said I'd find something important, something so important one man had already died trying to find it, and others had spent gobs of money to come here to look for it.

Propping myself on one elbow, the light held in the same hand, I could see the dark squarish shape against the lighter-colored beam. The whale-skin pouch.

Despite my lack of enthusiasm for my assignment, my heart began to beat a little faster, and I started to breathe a little harder. After all, this was a part of history, something worth getting excited about.

I felt like Nicolas Cage holding the Declaration of Independence in his hands in *National Treasure.* Pretty heady stuff.

Up close now I could see the whale-skin pouch Quincy had described was old and brittle. It had been nailed to the beam—the nail was solid rust, but it still held. The top flat of the pouch looked to be intact and closed. I shone the light around the thing, inspecting every inch of it.

My inspection came to a stop when I got a good look at the bottom of the pouch. It was shredded to the point of being nearly nonexistent. Ripped completely open.

I took my penlight, and using it as a tool at the bottom of the pouch, I separated the front of the pouch from the back. The beam of light lit up the inside—the *empty* inside. There was nothing there—nothing at all. Neither the leather document case nor Jean Lafitte's letter of pardon the mixed-race slave had stolen were there.

CHAPTER TEN

Quincy squinted at the monitor. "Can we see it again?"

Goodwin's cameraman hit the play switch for the third time, and the footage he'd shot of me inchworming my way over to the front of the house came up again. What there was of it anyway. The camera had only rolled on me a short way into my adventure.

Yep, there she is, folks—Melanie Hamilton skulking around in the sludge under the house like an oversized mudbug. Not your best moment, girl. Was Jack seeing this? I cringed.

Quincy took off his cap, scratched his head with the same hand, and then put the cap back on. "Dunno for sure, but it looks like to me somebody's been under there not too long ago. You can see older tracks like the ones Mel left under there. Elroy, maybe he did get in there and took that letter before he went sneaking around Mr. Villars' house, fell down, and killed hisself."

Harry, Nancy Villars, and Percy stood close by, eavesdropping. Percy kept shaking his head until he finally blurted out, "No. None of this makes any sense. My brother had the journal. We both knew the document was *under* the house, not *in* it. We were just waiting for Harry to get back home from his trip before we went looking for it. Why would Elroy have gone *to* the house much less *inside* it? And if he was the one who got to Lafitte's pardon first, then why would he tear the page from the journal and throw it away? Elroy knew that journal had to be kept intact. The advance from our publisher was contingent on a clean trail leading to the pardon. With all respect, Deputy, you're wrong about this. Really wrong."

Quincy cocked his head. "I admit I was wrong. Once. June 16, 2011. Wrong as I could be. We'd had this hellacious string of crab trap thefts. It went on for months and months. Man, every fisherman within eighty miles of here was losin' they catch. Dat thief was pretty smart. Turns out, smarter than me—but not for long. I bring in dis young guy after some bodacious police work, and then I charge him and toss him in the hoosegow. Then you know what? His mama, she come 'round and tell me it been her all the while, and she got the tools and the boat, and she even had some selfies proving it was her stealin' them crabs." He hung his head in shame. "I was wrong. It ain't been easy living it down." His head came back up. "But I got this one."

I had to admit, I pretty much agreed with Percy. Quincy's theory didn't hold together.

Quincy seemed to consider things before asking, "All right, Mr. Percy Villars, what do you think?"

Percy pulled himself up straight and tried to look like someone who should be taken seriously. It occurred to me that with his sweet, goofy face people probably disregarded him most of the time. Double that for when his twin brother was alive. I couldn't imagine what a big-time publisher would have thought when these two freckled gingers with enormous ears and foolish grins walked in claiming to be descendants of the notorious swashbuckling pirate, Jean Lafitte, and to be keepers of a secret journal that held the key to a document so valuable droves would search for it. It must have been a tough sell for the Villars twins, such a hard sell that the publisher demanded hard evidence.

So they'd come on down to NOLA and set out to follow the journal of Belle Villars to find the letter of pardon that would ultimately bestow fame and fortune on them.

But it had gone horribly wrong, and now Percy was left without his twin. "I don't believe my brother was in the house to steal anything. I don't know why he was there, but neither of us would have insulted Harry by breaking into his house—especially since we knew Belle hid the letter under the house. So, I'm not buying it that Elroy died by accident, and I'm not buying that he already had the letter. There's something else going on here, Deputy. And if you aren't up to finding out what it is"—he looked around at Nancy, Harry, and finally at me—"then maybe we are."

Harry picked up the gauntlet. "I truly believe that Belle Villars bore a child of Jean Lafitte and that her poor hurt soul lashed out at him by taking that letter of pardon which meant so much to him. I also believe that Percy and his unfortunate brother are my relations, by name and spirit if not by blood. And since I believe all this, if it turns out that poor young man was killed by someone's harsh hand, then I demand justice for him."

Quincy narrowed his eyes and looked from Percy to Harry to Nancy and then to me. "If the ME comes back and says Elroy's death was a homicide, then Jefferson Parrish Sheriff's Office goin' launch an official investigation. But not before. You wait for that. It's police business, and I don't want to hear 'bout you people goin' round sticking your noses in here like some"—he fixed his stare on me—"have been known to do in the past." He paused before adding, "You hear me?"

*　*　*

Since I was with Harry, I was one of the first to take the shuttle back to the main building. Fastidious Harry had the shuttle driver spread a pad on one of the seats where I could rest my muddy bum—which sounded like heaven to me. It had been one of the longest days I could recall. My morning work schedule, followed by the stress of Miss Man-stealing Hussy sniffing around Jack, the friendly neighborhood gator paying us a visit, the discovery of poor, dead Elroy in Harry and Fabrizio's bathroom, a busy afternoon of inking, spending the whole evening with the swamp rats, millipedes, cockroaches, and other creatures of the dark beneath *la petite maison*.

I could hardly wait to go to the room Harry had arranged for me where I'd shower and crash.

In the lobby I took possession of the room key at the front desk then turned back to find Harry and Fabrizio standing with Percy and Nancy Villars.

I walked up behind them just in time to hear Harry say, "It'll be over my dead body if any Villars dies by malicious means and the culprit isn't made to answer for it."

"It's kind of you to open your arms to us, Harry," Nancy said.

A distant gleam in his eye, Percy started to speak. "I keep expecting to look up and see Elroy walking toward me. I just can't—" He broke off, his voice cracking, his eyes glistening. Nancy took hold of his arm comfortingly.

Harry's brows lifted sympathetically. "I vow we'll get to the bottom of this, dear Percy."

Percy shook his head sadly and excused himself. We watched him walk away with his sister, his head hanging between hunched shoulders.

Harry's voice was quiet. "I worry that with this sort of thing seeming to happen more and more often around here that it won't be long before folks begin to think twice about paying us a visit."

He rubbed two fingers above his eyebrows.

It hadn't occurred to me before, but he was right. This wasn't the first time a dead body had turned up at The Mansion—although I did hope it would be the last—and how long before travelers began to think of Mystic Isle as murder central? I could hear the conversations now. *Darling, let's book a week in the bayou at Mystic Isle. Sure, sweetie. Is your will in order?*

If business slowed, how many of us would Harry have to lay off? Or could he even keep the place open if Frommer's travel guide suggested The Mansion at Mystic Isle could be *one of the last places you'll ever visit*?

The thought had me worried. Harry, Fabrizio, Jack, Cat, all my other friends, and not to forget about little ol' Melanie Hamilton were happy working at Mystic Isle. Jobs like those we had and bosses like ours were few and far between.

That worrying thought still in my head, I bid them all good night and made my way to my room. Quincy had been crossing the river to New Orleans twice a day to stay with Cat at our apartment on Dumaine Street. For the five years since I came to work at The Mansion at Mystic Isle and the four years Cat and I had been apartment mates, I'd known her to be a woman of fierce independent nature—the *never mind, I'll do it myself* kind of woman. It had surprised me when she'd come to me asking whether I had a problem with Quincy staying at our place while they were planning their wedding.

"I want him to help me with it," she'd said. "I *need* him to help me with it."

I'd recalled what people have always said about the wedding day being the biggest day of a woman's life. And although I'd never been sure that was true for everyone, it looked like it might actually be how things were for Cat.

I hadn't minded, not much anyway. I loved Quincy Boudreaux because Cat loved him, although I'd just about die before I let the cocky sonuva gun know it. But he could be hard to take in large doses, so I'd asked my Cap'n Jack if he minded if I played house with him in his cottage on the resort grounds while Cat and Quincy played house at our place.

He'd been so sweet. "Mind? I'd love it. Playing house with you is one of my life's ambitions."

And it had been great. Cuddling in front of the TV every evening, spooning at night, sharing a hot soapy shower in the morning. Great—until Florida when I'd gotten my feelings hurt and was having to work my way through that. Great—until Sydney Baxter had come on the scene and Jack wouldn't send her packing.

I stopped in front of the upstairs room, which I recognized as the same junior suite where I'd already been lucky enough to spend one night at the request of an important guest who'd been haunted.

Ha! A junior suite? Harry must really consider me his good luck charm.

I unlocked the door, stepped inside, and was carried back over a hundred and fifty years to a paradoxical time of crinolines and parasols, slavery and war. The king-size four-poster bed dominated the room, lush and inviting with its hand-sewn quilt and crocheted pillow covers. It was almost nine o'clock, and the fire housekeeping had built earlier in anticipation of my arrival was beginning to burn low. The velvet chaise at the foot of the bed had a fluffy robe and spa slippers laid across it. My suitcase sat on a luggage rack in one corner, leading me to wonder what Jack thought of my moving to the resort. *Oh, Jack. Jack. Jack.* But I was too tired to even think about that now.

I went straight to the en suite bathroom, stripped off the nasty old jumpsuit, and got into the steam shower. The stress flowed out of me and down the drain with the soapy water.

I found my sleep shirt, pulled back the covers on the enormous bed, and crawled in.

My mind turned to the day's events. To Harry, who believed a man had been murdered in his home, a man to whom he had a connection. Harry had vowed to see the killer brought to justice, but did that concern, in fact, outweigh his worry about the future of The Mansion if this matter wasn't quickly resolved?

Was he right? Had Elroy Villars been murdered? Quincy didn't seem to think so. Had someone else torn the page from the journal and gone looking for the historical letter? And if so, who? Was a murderer running loose at Mystic Isle? It wouldn't have been the first time.

And as I fell asleep, I acknowledged that I was already too involved not to jump right into the middle of all this.

Ah, Mellie gal, there you go again.

I sighed. "Goodnight, Granddaddy Joe. Wouldn't mind you keeping an eye on me if you can. Looks like I might be the designated homicide investigator around here."

I could have sworn I heard a chuckle.

CHAPTER ELEVEN

———

Two wooden sailing ships pitch in a rough ocean under a dark sky, one flying a foreign flag I don't recognize. On the other, the Jolly Roger flaps in the fierce wind. I'm aboard the foreign ship, locked in a cabin, being thrown side to side as the ship rolls. My elegant gown—pale and silky, ruffled and low-cut, exposing the mounds of a full bosom, the clothing of an aristocratic lady of the mid-1700s—is torn and dirty from the rough handling of my captors, slave-traders from the Far East. I rail and rant and pound on the door before being tossed back like a doll when the ship bucks yet again.

Above me, the grinding, shouting, and canon fire of a furious battle. A massive explosion. There's smoke everywhere, and I still can't escape the cabin. I scream and cry. The door shatters as it bursts inward, leaving a tall man framed in the opening. The ongoing battle rages on behind him. The dark clouds thunder above him.

The man is dressed in a tattered, billowy white shirt that appears to be smeared with grime and what might even be blood—the laces at the neck hang loose, exposing a hard chest. Tight leather pants hug his muscular legs, and cuffed black boots rise to his knees. I stand and stare at him, at the flintlock pistol tucked into the wide sash tied low around his waist, at the scabbard at his side, the cutlass held in the hand he's using to prop himself against the doorframe. A gold earring nestles against long and dark hair curling under a red scarf tied around his head that I recognize as my own. The pirate—for I now know that's what he is—swaggers into the cabin. At first I back away, breathing hard, bosom heaving, my eyes locked onto his as he advances on me like a big cat. But at last I fling myself against his hard chest and hold fast to him. Amaretto eyes glitter down at me from within a rugged countenance as a cocky grin spreads across his handsome face.

"Oh," I breathe. "Cap'n Jack. I knew you'd come."

He lowers his head, and our mouths collide as he lifts me with one arm, carries me out onto the deck, and we swing across from the foreign ship to the pirate ship just like Tarzan and Jane.

His feet hit the deck, but he doesn't release me as he barks, "Avast ye. Make way for Barataria Bay."

He pulls me down to his cabin, his eyes burning into mine as he unstraps his scabbard, lays his pistol on the table, and walks toward me, his taut frame speaking his intention louder than words ever could.

I'd sat straight up in bed, surprised to see the Sunday morning sun coming through the shutters that I'd forgotten to close the night before. A glance at the bedside clock told me it was after nine a.m. My face was still hot as I remembered the dream, my breathing still rapid, body still wanting. Wanting him.

What a dream. What a man. Cap'n Jack Stockton. Wow. He'd fit my fantasy to perfection. No wonder it had taken me a few minutes to remember when or where I was right away.

But then I did remember—the tragic death of Elroy Villars, the horrible journey through the mire under *la petite maison*, the issue over Jack, his mom, and his ex. Saturday had been terrible.

I lay back and sank down into the comfortable cocoon of the four-poster, pulling the soft sheets and quilt up to my chin. A chill had set in during the night. The fire had long since gone out, and I'd forgotten to set the thermostat before hitting the sack, but the bed was warm. It would have been so nice on my day off to just hang out in the junior suite, order one of Chef Valentine Cantrell's awesome Southern brunches—but the cogs were already turning, and the mystery was already jabbing away at my brain like a boxer at a punching bag.

What had happened to Elroy Villars? Had he fallen on his own, hitting his head—accidental death as Quincy thought? And what about the all-important document? Why wasn't it where it had been hidden centuries ago? Had Elroy retrieved it?

If so, where was it now? Percy was adamant his brother would have never defaced the journal by ripping out a page nor would he have broken into Harry's house. Yet the page had been ripped out, Elroy had died in Harry's home, and Jean Lafitte's letter had disappeared.

Huh. Looked like there was more than one mystery to solve—or was there? Did all the pieces fit together to solve one big puzzle?

I swung my feet over the side of the bed, dressed in clean clothes from my suitcase, called Percy Villars' room, and made arrangements to meet him on the terrace outside The Presto-Change-o Room where they served chicory coffee and warm beignets until eleven.

Percy knew more than anyone else about everything that happened both in the past and the present. Besides, if any of the shows I watched on TV were even a teensy-tiny bit accurate, if in fact Elroy had been killed by the hand of some evildoer, the family was the first place to look. Talking to Percy was definitely an excellent place to begin.

The air was cool, and the morning sun was bright but dappled through the live oaks shading the terrace crowded with guests. The feel of autumn was in the air. Even in the bayou there's a change of season—more subtle than in other parts of the country but there all the same.

I waited until one of the waiters cleared a table then sat and ordered the basic staples: two café au laits, two orders of beignets. I sipped my coffee but held off on the beignets—hard as it was, I didn't want to begin my investigation into the death of Elroy Villars with powdered sugar all over my face—and hoped Percy would come soon.

He walked up to the table. "Hello, Miss Hamilton."

"Call me Mel," I said. "Please, sit down."

The night hadn't treated him well. He looked pale with dark circles under his eyes, deep lines where his reddish brows nearly met and around his wide mouth. He grimaced at the au lait coffee I'd ordered for him and signaled the waiter, asking for a fresh cup. "Black, please."

"Black? You ever had plain ol' chicory coffee?" I asked. "You might not like it much."

Percy nodded as the waiter returned, pouring him a fresh cup from a small silver coffee urn. He blew on it then sipped. "I like it better this way." Obviously not a man of the true South. Everyone knew half chicory coffee and half steamed milk was the way to go.

"How are you holding up?" I asked.

He lowered his eyes and shook his head. "I never expected to be without my brother at this stage of my life. I mean, we were in the womb together for heaven's sake. And now"—he paused, seeming to be at a loss for words—"he's just…gone."

I nodded, feeling his pain, his loss. I didn't say anything else. Words would have been paltry.

He sniffed a couple of times before looking up and around then checking out the beignets, picking one up, and taking a bite. He closed his eyes when he chewed. "These are pretty darn good."

I jumped on it, glad for the chance to take his mind off Elroy's death. "Percy, do you mind talking to me about your brother's death and the missing letter?"

His gaze was direct. "No. I don't mind. I'm glad to talk about it. That sheriff's deputy? He's wrong. Someone killed Elroy and stole the letter. That letter was our legacy."

"Is there anything you can add to what I already know that might help me look into it? I know Harry wants to figure all this out, but I feel like he'll need quite a bit of help. Harry's not cut out to deal with this kind of thing." How could I explain the kind and gentle man my friend Fabrizio had come to love without making him sound like a wimp?

"I can see that," Percy said. "Harry's cut from a different kind of cloth, isn't he? Like a man from a simpler time. More genteel."

I was surprised at Percy's accurate perception. "Yes. Harry is just that."

"Okay. What to tell you. Hmm, well, you know about Belle and the love affair. You know about the letter and why she took it. Hell, that letter would probably sell to a museum for several hundred thousand dollars, maybe more."

I whistled. Like all my whistles, it was kind of lame and windy. But that was a lot of money for a piece of paper.

Percy went on. "You also know why we've come down here to look for it—"

I stopped him. "Yeah, about that. You said you and your brother had a book deal and couldn't collect your advance until you came up with the letter to prove the tale of Belle and her pirate is legit, that it really happened."

He swallowed the bite of beignet then took a sip of his black coffee, making me grimace. I could only tolerate black chicory coffee if I'd indulged in too many hurricanes the night before.

"That's right," he said. "It's a generous advance."

"Generous?" I asked.

"$250,000. The publisher was excited about our book, said a story this rich in history and scandal would sell millions of copies. But Elroy and I couldn't collect until we'd proved ourselves. Well, you know that part."

"You and your brother? Your sister isn't part of the book deal?"

He shook his head. "Oh, no. Our sister was adopted. She's not a true descendent of Lafitte." He grew sad again. "But now that our parents and Elroy are all dead, she's all the family I have. Blood relative or not."

"She seems to know a lot about your family history."

"She's taken quite an interest in it. I'll need her now to help out with the book—research, stuff like that. I'd pay her, of course, but the book will officially be authored by the Villars twins, Percy and Elroy." He stopped talking for a moment and looked away. "Well, now just Percy Villars."

"You're going ahead with it?" I asked, a little surprised.

"Well, yeah," he said. "Elroy would want it. And why wouldn't I? That is, if I can find the lost letter."

"Then you'd get all the income from the book." A minimum of $250,000.00 is a lot of money. A lot of motive.

He looked at me like I was an idiot. "Now that my brother's gone, yes."

Commotion at the far end of the terrace interrupted us as first the rogue alligator then Lurch, Odeo, and the rest of the

Gator Brigade scurried single file through Harry's hard-won rose garden, sending guests scattering for cover.

"That's amazing," Percy said.

I agreed. "It is." I had one more question. "Now that your brother's"—I searched for a diplomatic word—"passed on, will you be bringing your sister onboard to take a bigger role in getting this book to market?"

Percy screwed up his round face as he seemed to be thinking about it. "Well, that's one option, I guess."

"Do you think she'd be willing to help you?"

"Nancy? Are you kidding? She'd love it. She already had her nose out of joint because Elroy and I were splitting that big paycheck from the book, and she was pretty much left out of things."

"You'd ask her even though she isn't a blood descendent of Jean Lafitte?" I asked.

"I'd be the only legitimate heir, but if my sister took over Elroy's role, helping with the writing, doing legwork, that stuff? Hell, yeah, I'd split the money with her. Nancy'd jump at the chance to take over Elroy's role."

Jump? How high? High enough to kill her own brother?

CHAPTER TWELVE

———

Percy didn't seem to want to answer any more of my questions and began deflecting mine with several of his own. They mostly centered around Harry Villars, but I didn't feel comfortable sharing personal information about Harry, so I was evasive. When the conversation lagged, Percy checked the time and stood.

"I better get going, check in on Nancy. She's taking Elroy's death as hard as I am."

Really? I hadn't thought so.

Our attention was drawn through the wide-open terrace doors as two men, one tall and lanky, the other shorter and stout rushed into the Presto-Change-o Room and stopped dead. I thought of Gandalf and Frodo. The taller one carried a newspaper, which he unfolded. Both men took a few seconds to look at something in the paper. Then they looked up and around, their heads moving back and forth in some kind of search mode. Gandalf looked down at Frodo, pointed to the far end of the room. Frodo nodded, hurried over to the stage, and began to shove the musicians' chairs aside. Gandalf headed in the opposite direction toward the restroom facilities.

From behind the bar, Ken, the bartender and morning shift headwaiter, yelled at the hostess. His voice carried all the way out to where we sat on the terrace. "Gotta be more of those treasure hunters."

Over by the entrance, the hostess pointed in Gandalf's direction as he ran into the ladies' room. "I'll get that one," she said loudly and took off.

Ken tossed his towel down and scrambled from behind the bar. "Sir, please stop that." He was yelling at the short intruder who'd opened the top of the upright piano. "Sir, you can't be doing that. You hear?"

I watched, astonished. "What the heck?"

Percy seemed to know all about it. "There was a big article in the morning paper about what's happened here"—his voice softened—"to Elroy and about Jean Lafitte and the letter. *Historical treasure worth a fortune,* the article said. This whole place is swarming with fortune seekers this morning."

I stared at him.

"You didn't know?" he asked.

I shook my head. I'd been too tired to watch the news last night and too preoccupied to read the paper this morning.

A couple of other anxious-looking people bustled out onto the terrace, followed closely by one of the bellmen who stopped them and politely directed them back out to the lobby.

"I don't know what to think," I said.

Percy just shook his head. "They're all fools. Someone else already has the letter. The more I think about it, the more I believe Elroy died—no, I believe he was killed—before he could get it. I believe that as we sit here talking, as these people scurry around trying to be the lucky ones to discover the letter, someone else already has it."

His theory made sense to me. Twins, especially identical twins, are said to be linked in ways no other human beings are.

Quincy always said to look at close family first, but in this case it didn't make sense—at least to me. Why would Percy want me to help Harry find who killed his brother if it had been him? No, I didn't think Percy was involved, and besides, Quincy wasn't even investigating Elroy's death. I was.

Percy excused himself and walked away, his steps heavy, his shoulders slumped. I felt terrible for him. He must be so lonely without his twin brother, like someone had cut out a piece of him. But as I watched him leave the terrace by way of the Presto-Change-o Room, I considered what had occurred to me when I'd first spoken with him. What if he *had* killed his brother and taken the letter from under the house so he wouldn't have to share the money and the fame from the guaranteed bestselling book? What if his desire to find the heartless killer *was* all a smokescreen and Percy was setting up someone else to be the fall guy—or fall girl?

I ate all the beignets, including those he'd left untouched, got up, and paid the bill, grateful for my employee discount.

I stopped and stretched before stepping through the double doors that led from the Presto-Change-o Room into the lobby but only took a couple of steps before stopping to stare, slack jawed, at what was going on.

The lobby was as packed as Bourbon Street during Mardi Gras—well, okay, maybe not that packed, but busier than I'd ever seen it in the five years I'd worked there.

At the front desk, poor Lucy looked like she might be losing her mind. People were lined up six or eight deep and all demanding her attention by trying to shout at her over the others. Lucy's normally tidy appearance and clockwork efficiency had both disappeared. Her hair, styled in an Uma Thurman *Pulp Fiction* perfect bob, usually smooth as glass, looked like it was full of static electricity, as if she'd just pulled a sweater over her head. Her magazine-ad eye makeup was smeared. Her lips didn't look as if they'd ever met a tube of lipstick. Not to mention her resort costume, an old-fashioned shirtwaist and long black skirt, looked as if she'd been sleeping in it. The high collar on the shirt was unbuttoned, the string tie hanging loose. She bustled from one side of the desk to the other, answering questions for one person then the next.

As the crowd moved and shifted nearly in sync, Lurch, loaded down with bags, bobbed and weaved through clusters of people, his arms lifting and lowering, his torso turning and twisting, every bit as graceful as a *Swan Lake* soloist, only bigger—much bigger. His face its usual stony, unreadable mask.

Where had all these people come from? Were they really all here to search for Jean Lafitte's letter? I'd obviously underestimated its lure to the general public.

Over by the double doors that led to the salon, Theresa Powell stood watching the goings-on, her pretty face set in a scowl. She was dressed the same way as I'd seen her before.

I walked over to her. "Quite a shindig, isn't it?"

She just looked at me, deadpan.

I stuck out my hand. "Melanie Hamilton. I work here. I saw you last night at the little house. I was the one who—"

"Oh, yes." She accepted my offered hand, her grip cool and surprisingly firm. "You're the adventuress who volunteered to wriggle around in the mud beneath the house to look for the letter." She sighed. "The missing letter. The missing letter all these people are determined to find."

"You don't think they'll find it?"

She shook her head.

"Why not?" I asked. "Do you think someone already has it? That someone took it from where the Villars' journal said it was hidden?"

"Archie and I know the letter exists. It's in the history books. We know about Belle Villars and her genealogy. That's also been documented. What we don't know is whether that letter has been in the same place under the house all this time." She looked out over the chaotic lobby and shook her head again. "There ought to be a law, don't you think? These things should be left to professionals. Otherwise, this"—she displayed her contempt with a wave of her hand—"is what you get. Idiots with metal detectors and shovels. Metal detectors? I mean, come on. It's a letter, not a watch or a set of car keys. Simpletons think they'll find the letter and make a killing selling it off."

"You wouldn't sell it if you found it?"

"Absolutely not. Archie and I had planned to keep it to put on display at our flagship store in Boston. Once we're established as bankable archeologists and finders of antiquities, our plans are to use the prestige of such a find as a stepping stone to expanding our business countrywide, becoming a brand name. You know, like McDonald's?"

I nodded as if I knew what she was talking about. At the very least, I could always say I had heard of McDonald's. Next to Café du Monde, it was my go-to breakfast spot—but I wouldn't want my mom or grandmamma to find out. They'd have a stroke. They're pretty sure if you don't have beignets for breakfast, it better be grillades and grits, or pain perdu, hot boudin and cracklins, or if there's time to make the hollandaise, eggs Sardou. I was pretty sure Egg McMuffins weren't on their hot list of haute cuisine.

At that moment, the funeral dirge sounded, and the crowd by the front door parted in such a fashion I expected Moses and the Israelites to come striding through. It turned out to be the cameraman who'd filmed my butt while I was under Harry and Fabrizio's house. He was with Roger "Mr. Hollywood" Goodwin, and they were both walking in backwards.

After Roger Goodwin and the cameraman came one of the film crew members holding a boom mic then finally Archie Powell. Mr. Powell was talking as he walked, making grand gestures with his hands, obviously a man who basked in the spotlight. He wore that same safari-style outfit I'd seen on the news. It made me wonder if those were the only outfits the Powells owned. Maybe the antiquities biz didn't pay as well as I'd thought.

Archie Powell and the entourage halted a few steps inside. Archie stopped his soliloquy, and Roger Goodwin sang out, "Cut. That's a take."

Archie's sweeping gaze found Theresa, and he came to us, bending to rub Theresa's bare arm and plant a kiss on her upturned cheek. When he stood back from her, he extended a hand and spoke to me. "Hello, Miss…" He had this musical voice that made the simple greeting sound like he was amused by it.

"Oh, sorry," Theresa said. "Archie, this is Melanie Hamilton. You remember from last night? She was the one they sent under the—"

"Oh, yes." His odd, colorless eyes crinkled at the corners as he caught my hand between the two of his. "Great show, Miss Hamilton. I have to admit I got caught up in the drama of it all."

"It turned out to be a waste of time." I shrugged. "You've probably heard there was nothing under there."

He nodded. "Mmm, it was a bit of a Geraldo Rivera moment, wasn't it?"

Theresa turned to me. "We're continuing on as if last night never happened."

"Oh? In what way?"

Archie opened his mouth to speak, but it was Roger Goodwin who answered. "Archie and Theresa are continuing to work on the documentary with me and my crew, continuing to seek out the lost letter of Lafitte. By the way, that's what we're calling the film, you know, *The Lost Letter of Jean Lafitte*. Brilliant, don't you think?"

"Sure," I said. "Catchy." But I was puzzled. "So you don't think someone's already found it—as in killed Mr. Villars, ripped the page from the journal, crawled under the house, and removed the hidden document?"

Theresa started to speak, but Archie laid his hand on her arm, effectively shushing her.

"How can any of us be certain the letter was ever there to begin with? We prefer to believe it's still out there somewhere." Archie's statement echoed his wife's earlier one, and he reached up to grip Roger Goodwin's shoulder. "We've already spent so much money documenting our quest by hiring the film crew. Theresa and I will continue to seek out the presidential pardon doc, and we believe we'll ultimately prevail and be able to show the world that real live heroes still live in this world." He lifted his chin, a faraway look in his eyes. "Archie and Theresa Powell will become household names written in the annals of history, and our star will rise like a beacon in the night—especially if the right person sees us on film, and we can sign on to a reality show."

"Man," Roger Goodwin said. "What a shame the cameras weren't rolling to record that. It was magnificent, Archie. Just magnificent."

Without saying it out loud, I totally agreed with Mr. Hollywood. What a shame the cameras weren't rolling. Acting like that, or more accurately *over*acting like that, shouldn't go unrecorded.

"Do you remember what you said?" Roger asked. "I mean, exactly?" We could go out on the veranda. You too, Theresa." He made a camera frame with his hands. "We could get a shot of Archie making that little speech. Theresa, you could cling to his arm, the two of you looking off at the horizon. Whew, magic. But maybe drop the remark about the reality show," he finished.

"Yeah, I remember," Archie said.

Roger went for his cell phone and motioned for Archie and Theresa to follow him. "Get the guys back out on the veranda to set up another shot," he barked into the phone.

Archie and Theresa turned to follow Mr. Hollywood. Archie stopped and said, "So nice to have met you, Miss Hamilton. A real pleasure."

I returned his smile, wondering if the Powells' drive to be famous beyond the academic world was so intense it might have driven them to attack Elroy Villars and snatch the letter. It was something to think about. After all, they were proceeding with the documentary film as if the letter hadn't been taken from beneath the house, as if they still had a chance to find it themselves. Not such an unlikely occurrence if they already had it.

Over at the front desk, the calm, authoritative presence of the hot-as-a-five-alarm-fire Jack Stockton seemed to be soothing the crowd surging around the front desk.

I stood there watching him, missing him. In the time we'd been together, he'd never given me cause to doubt him. What was it about what had happened in Florida and the arrival of Sydney Baxter that had turned me into a jealous child? His mother's rejection hadn't been his fault, and Sydney showing up and crawling all over him hadn't been either. Yet, Jack was the misguided target of my anger.

Silly, Mel. Don't just stand there pining for his company. Do something about it.

I intended to.

CHAPTER THIRTEEN

———

Accompanied by the low and mournful funeral dirge, I walked through the lobby doors onto the expansive front veranda and stood looking out over the lawn. I was astounded to finally witness just exactly how sought after President Madison's pardon truly was. The sun was bright, the sky clear, the October breeze cooler than it had been in a while. The feeling of fall was in the air, even in the bayou—and people rushed about here and there, hither and yon like a swarm of tweens at a Justin Bieber sighting, or were clustered together over a newspaper akin to an NFL team in huddle.

The Mystic Isle shuttle pulled up under the portico, opened its doors, and disgorged a full load of people, most of whom carried at least a newspaper with them and literally hit the ground running.

Bogged down with several suitcases, Lurch lumbered out onto the veranda. He'd been preceded by three couples who stood looking out over the same bizarre scene that I was.

"Really?" one woman said in a disgusted tone.

"Not what we came here for anyway," added a second woman.

"Too much going on." It was one of the men.

"Can't get away from here fast enough for me." The third woman turned and motioned for Lurch to follow them down the steps and out to the shuttle.

Not good. Not good for business, not at all. Something had to be done to get The Mansion back on even keel. We had to find both the killer and the letter.

I stopped, realizing what thought had just run through my head. *Even keel?* This pirate business might have been affecting me more than I thought.

"What you think 'bout all this ruckus?"

I turned to look Quincy Boudreaux square in his big brown peepers. "To be honest, I don't know what to think."

Quincy stood by me, his arms crossed over his chest, his cap pulled low on his brow. "It's a sight," he said.

I had to ask. "Are all these people really here to look for that letter?"

He shrugged. "I guess. It's been all over the papers and TV. It's really somethin', it is."

"And you don't think with all this hullaballoo that somebody might have wanted it badly enough to have fought with Elroy Villars to find out where it was hidden and killed him in the process?"

He clicked his teeth, his eyes on the pond where it looked like Odeo was trying to shoo a few enthusiastic treasure hunters away from the boathouse.

"The coroner still thinks dat man, he die accidental from hitting his poor head on Harry's nice big clawfoot tub in *la petite maison*." I always loved it when Quincy spoke French in his Cajun accent. It was just so cool. "Until the coroner tell me different, Elroy Villars died from being a klutz."

"But, Q, don't you want to know what happened to Jean Lafitte's letter?" Seemed to me that a true detective wouldn't be able to resist a mystery this juicy.

Again, that lazy shrug that didn't match the shrewd look in his eye. "Nah, it don't matter to me. Nobody said yet it truly belonged to them. Nobody asked the Sheriff to find out who took it."

"I think if we find the letter, we might find out more about who or what killed Elroy Villars."

He took his index finger and pushed his cap back on his head. Amusement was in the crinkle of his eyes. "It sound to me like maybe you don't put much in store by what our good coroner has to say 'bout dis."

What could I say? He was right. What Percy had told me about how the journal was all but sacrosanct to his brother as well as the fact that Elroy had broken into Harry's house when the letter wasn't even supposed to be there, well, it just made me skeptical about Quincy and the parish coroner's version of the events that led to Elroy's death.

"If there's no official investigation, what are you doing here on Sunday morning?" I asked.

"Things are so busy hereabouts, they asked my Kitty Cat to come on in and work. She got a break round eleven, so I'm gonna buy her some coffee and a coupla beignets before I check in at the office. You wanna come too?"

"No thanks. You two lovebirds need your alone time." I made a couple of kissy sounds. "And besides, I'm pretty sure Fabrizio needs to talk to me."

Fabrizio had come up behind Quincy while we were talking and stood there making hand gestures, indicating he really wanted to see me. When Quincy turned around and walked away, Fabrizio hotfooted it right on over, put his arm around my shoulders, and steered me to the far end of the veranda.

"Good morning, Fabrizio," I said.

He stood beside me, his gaze slightly alarmed as he took in the constant activity going on around us.

"Harry tells me this"—his hand lifted to indicate all the rushing around everyone was doing—"all this is a dichotomy for The Mansion. On the one hand, all these treasure hunters will probably be patronizing our bars and cafés, maybe dropping by the gift shops—an economic boon. On the other hand, the disruption is upsetting the actual resort guests who are trying to book appointments with the cast, have a quiet hour or two in the spa"—he pointed at a middle-aged couple sitting down a ways from us on the veranda in the process of picking up their coffee and moving inside—"those two for instance. It won't take long for the basic amenities to be somewhat neglected because staff is being pulled away from assigned duties."

I thought of Odeo trying to shoo a small group away from the boathouse only moments ago and the three couples who'd just left on the shuttle.

He went on. "Harry and your Jack"—my breath caught at the mention of Jack's name, *my* Jack—"have sent word to the sheriff's office, asking if perhaps some of their off-duty personnel could come 'round to help out with this influx of humanity."

I smiled. "Influx of humanity. That's what it is all right." When he didn't respond, I asked, "You acted like you needed to talk to me. So what's up?" Since obviously something was.

"I'm afraid I've become quite nervous regarding this matter of Percy and Nancy Villars." He shook his head, and I could see he truly was bothered.

"Nervous? How?" I laid my hand on his arm.

"I cherish Harry," he began, and I smiled. "I would never want to see him hurt or taken unfair advantage of, not by anyone."

"Of course not," I said.

"I find myself wondering if perhaps these Villars people aren't somehow trying to…" He paused and seemed to be searching for just the right word. "Scam—that's it—scam him. I've been doubting their veracity and worrying they might be trying to somehow scam Harry into believing they're related to him."

"But they're not related, not by blood," I said. "Their ancestor was a slave who went by the family name. Surely Harry knows that. It seemed very clear to me."

"Oh, he knows it. But you know how my Harry is, generous to a fault. I just don't want him to make a connection to these people only to somehow be hurt by them. I don't suppose you'd be amenable to checking into their background a bit, would you? Just to be sure they are who they claim to be?"

So that's what he was about.

Well, why not? I had already said I'd help Harry find out what really went down the night Elroy died. It would be a simple matter to check out the history of Percy's branch of the Villars family while I was at it. "I can do that," I said. "No problem."

And with that, the forlorn expression on Fabrizio's face disappeared, and he hugged me before setting me back at arms' length. "Thank you, my dear. You're one of the best friends I've ever had."

The Great Fabrizio, one of The Mansion at Mystic Isle's most popular cast members, conducted *séances* by appointment in a special room that had been perfectly designed for that purpose. That day he was dressed for work in monochromatic steel blue from the turban with the enormous fake diamond to his boots and everything in between.

"Did you get called in for work too?" I asked. "Quincy said Cat had been asked to come in."

Fabrizio nodded. "It seems the Powells have booked a *séance* for the purpose of asking those beyond the veil to locate this infamous missing letter. They're going to have it recorded by those movie people." He said the word *movie* like it was the nauseating castor oil my Grandmamma Ida used to force on me when I'd overindulged on Pixy Stix and made myself sick.

"So looks like you're going to be a movie star," I teased him. "Are you still going to talk to us peons when you're rich and famous?"

He pulled a skeptical expression. "This old thespian? My dear, I don't believe that's likely to be an issue."

With that, he turned and walked away, tossing back over his shoulder. "Ta-ta for now." Always the consummate actor, he spun, threw back his head, and gave me an awesome Gloria Swanson. "Mr. Hollywood, I'm ready for my close-up."

* * *

Back in the lobby, I managed to flag down Lucy from dealing with the mob. Jack was nowhere to be seen at that point, probably called away to some other part of the resort.

Poor Lucy looked so hassled. My heart went out to her.

"When does your shift end?" I asked.

She shook her head. "Not soon enough."

"Miss? Miss?" The call came from a tall woman standing at the front desk banging on Harry's old-fashioned counter bell. Between that, the general roar of people talking and moving about, and the funeral dirge playing whenever someone came through the front doors, it was bedlam.

Lucy put her hands over her ears. "Keep going, lady. Maybe you'll break the stupid bell." She looked at me. "That would be one good thing we get out of all this, wouldn't it?"

I nodded my agreement even though I'd always thought the bell was sort of charming. Of course it wasn't my job to hang out at the front desk and listen to it through every shift. "Have you seen Nancy Villars this morning? I'd like to talk to her."

Lucy's whole demeanor changed. "Oh, the poor thing." Both her tone and expression were suddenly sympathetic. "She came by here asking if there was someplace quiet where she could meditate. I sent her to Harry's Garden, you know out back of the resort where they're building the water feature?" Her head swiveled as the clamor over by her station rose again. "But the way things are going around here this morning, I'm betting it's not even quiet there."

The clamor behind us rose again.

"I gotta go," she said apologetically then laughed. "My public wants me."

I laughed too. "Thanks, Lucy. I'll go have a look in the garden."

Harry's Garden was the one place at the resort where the paranormal was banned. The center of it was quite formal with walkways of brick pavers and grass so well-manicured if even one single blade was a millimeter longer than any of the others, it'd be noticeable. That area was lined with formal beds planted with palmettos and low shrubbery in some areas and flowering plants in others. Ornate French-style wrought iron benches with colorful cushions sat in strategic spots with good views of the garden, the surrounding grounds and buildings, and the wild areas of the bayou beyond. Harry's beautiful roses took up almost one entire side of the area. A Japanese-style wooden bridge crossed over a koi pond, while a white gingerbread-trimmed gazebo graced the center area.

The perimeter of the garden was more informal where Spanish moss hung from live oak trees and purple, white, blue, and yellow wildflowers had been left to flourish. Odeo took an enormous amount of pride in Harry's Garden and kept it in immaculate shape. He'd been dismayed when an area of it had been dug up to begin construction on the water feature Harry was having built at one end of the garden. The barricades, temporary fencing, and screening would be in place until the project was finished. It was scheduled to be done in time for Cat and Quincy to be married in front of it.

It was going to be a beautiful wedding.

As I maneuvered my way through the garden, I spotted Nancy Villars seated on one of the benches. She was slumped forward, her head in her hands.

It was crummy to impose on her, and I had started to turn around when she looked up and saw me.

"Hello," she said quietly.

I stopped and turned toward her. "Hi, Nancy."

"Hello."

"May I join you?" I asked.

She nodded, so I went and sat beside her, taking the time to push one of the patio pillows behind the small of my back.

We sat at least a full minute or two without speaking before she said, "It's so lovely out here."

"You must miss your brother very much."

She looked up at me with tired eyes. "I do. Of course I wasn't as close to Elroy as Percy. I'm sure he's even more devastated than I am by all this. You can't understand the way the twins related to each other unless you've lived with them, watched them together. It was eerie. It was a bond like no other. No matter what came between them, no matter how angry they might have been with one another, there was always the bond"—her voice took on a slightly harsher tone—"the *twins* thing."

"Percy told me about their book deal, about how it all hinged on their coming up with proof of their lineage and validation of the journal by coming up with Lafitte's letter."

"It was why we came here. I'm thinking Percy probably wishes he'd never heard of Jean Lafitte. I'm thinking he's probably going to get in touch with the publisher and call the whole thing off after"—she faltered—"after what's happened."

It was the opening I'd been waiting for. "I don't think so. I saw Percy this morning, and he said he planned on going through with the book deal and that he hoped you'd help him with it. Said he planned to pay you if you would."

A look of surprise came over her. "He said that?"

"Yes. You aren't interested in helping him?"

"Oh my God, yes. I've wanted to help them ever since the beginning of this whole thing—ever since our mother gave them the journal—ever since they embarked on this great adventure." She looked away, a tad bit starry-eyed.

"Wow," I said.

"What do you mean, 'Wow?'"

I shrugged. "I don't know, you just seem really excited about something that sounds more like a lot of work than a 'great adventure.' Guess I'm just surprised."

She stood and crossed her arms over her chest. Defensive. "A girl like me looks at something such as this as a great adventure."

"A girl like you?"

"My life's been pretty bland. If there was something my adoptive parents needed done, I was the one they looked to for help. Not the boys. Never the boys."

Oh, right. Cinderella complex. Bibbidi-bobbidi-boo. "Really?" I prodded.

"Don't get me wrong. They loved me, and I loved them, and I really loved the boys. I sheltered them every bit as much as Mom and Dad did. I mean, how adorable are they anyway?" She kind of laughed before sobering. "Were, I guess. How adorable were they…I mean." She shook it off. "Besides, if he plans on paying me, I have a great use for some extra cash."

"Yeah?" When she didn't answer right away, I added in a teasing voice, "I could probably conjure up a pretty special tattoo for any extra cash you come up with."

She laughed. It was small, but it was still a laugh. "Thanks, but I think I'll pass. I have something different in mind. Some*one* different in mind. A certain someone."

Ah-ha. A man. When a woman says a certain someone with that kind of look in her eye, she's talking about a man. "You have a boyfriend?"

She frowned and looked irritated that I'd asked her. "Well, why not? Not every man is looking for Jennifer Lopez."

Oops. "No, that's not what I meant at all. I was just making conversation."

She snorted and walked a few paces away, her jaw set, her chin in the air.

A soft breeze rattled the palm fronds and swayed the Spanish moss. "Harry and Odeo have done a beautiful job out here. Don't you think?"

She seemed quieter, calmer. "It's beautiful. I wouldn't mind staying here."

I thought back to what Fabrizio had said about them trying to move in on Harry. "Stay here?"

"I was only speaking figuratively, of course. My life's back in Chicago. I'm a big-city girl."

Another moment passed when neither of us spoke, and then I ventured. "Something's been bothering me about Elroy's—about what happened."

She looked at me, waiting.

"If Elroy had the journal and knew where the document was supposedly hidden, why would he go there alone to get it? I mean, I had the impression the twins were practically inseparable and were in this"—I coined her term—"*adventure* together all the way. Why wouldn't he have taken Percy with him?"

She didn't even pause to take a breath. "He wouldn't have. You're right. Elroy would never have gone near the place without Percy in tow. When it came to the journal, the letter, this whole thing, they might as well have been Siamese twins—they were that joined at the hip. Elroy just wouldn't have gone to look for the letter without…"

I waited a long beat before asking, "So are you saying you think the two *were* together at *la petite maison*, at Harry's? If they were, that would mean Percy was with Elroy when…" I let it hang, not anxious to say the word murder.

Nancy picked up on what I said right away, a look of horror taking over her face. "Oh, no. Oh my God, no. I didn't think about… I didn't mean he"—then finally—"Just plain *no*. He wouldn't."

She stared at me.

I didn't know exactly what to say. All I had to offer was a lame, "Of course not." But something had obviously drawn Elroy to *la petite maison*. Was that something his brother?

She was breathing hard, and her cheeks had gone awfully pink. She pushed her limp hair back off her forehead and looked around, probably for the quickest path leading away from me.

"Well, I have to go," she said. "Have to…uh…" She stopped and seemed to be searching her repertoire for a good excuse to leave but finally just shrugged and said, "Good-bye."

I watched her obvious state of distress and confusion, and I almost felt bad about what I'd encouraged her to say.

Nancy's voice quivered. "Pretend I never said anything. Please. I'm just, well, upset. I'm sure you understand."

She turned and walked away.

Percy had seemed like a pretty nice guy, one who cared about his family. And now he had a connection to Harry, whom *I* cared about. I didn't want Percy to be the one. But now I had to wonder. Did Nancy know something that had led her to think the twins had been together at *la petite maison*?

Pretend I never said anything? I almost wished I could, but it wasn't going to happen. No way she could take it back or that I could unhear what she'd already said.

The cat was out of the bag. It was an ugly one at that, and I was pretty sure all the catnip in the world wouldn't entice that kitty back in the sack.

CHAPTER FOURTEEN

———

Her timing couldn't have been more perfect. Her exit was nearly simultaneous to an almost military-style assault on the garden by a small group of treasure hunters, checking their maps of the resort against the newspaper.

They flew by me, chattering among themselves.

Close on their heels came Odeo and two of his groundskeepers. *Lord have mercy*, as Grandmamma Ida would say. God help the fortune hunters if they so much as even bruised one poppy or flattened one blade of grass. Odeo's posture and the look in his eye as he rushed past me reminded me of a mother bear with a cub in peril. *Be careful, people.*

Back in the lobby things had actually calmed down some. It was getting close to lunchtime, and if my guess was correct, the Presto-Change-o Room and outdoor venues where Sunday brunch and early lunch were being served were probably standing room only.

Coming through the front entrance to the tune of the funeral dirge was Chief Deputy Quincy Boudreaux accompanied by a half dozen—no, there were eight—other deputies. Quincy stopped beside me, but the others moved on, fanning out in different directions.

"Hey," he said.

"What's all this?" I asked.

"I was just leaving here when I got a call that Elroy Villars' cause of death wasn't accidental. Bludgeoned to death." He shook his head, eyes squinted, mouth twisted. "Eww. Bad way to buy dat farm."

When you're right, you're right. "Bludgeoned?"

"Something heavy. So, we're here now, all us deputies, and probably you're gonna see us here awhile. Because we got us a homicide. Elroy Villars, he was beat to death."

I just stared at him.

He went on. "So now I'm on my way to tell Jack we're ready to help him get all these crazy people loaded on the shuttle and bussed outta here. Then we can get down to some good ol' fashioned police work."

He gave me a mock salute. Those warm brown eyes were alive with enthusiasm. Chief Deputy Boudreaux was in his element. "Catch ya later."

So the sheriff was finally on board with homicide. That was a good thing for Harry, who had taken this pretty hard, and justice for Elroy's death would probably make him feel better about it all. His home had been the scene of a murder. How must that have felt to him? I couldn't even begin to imagine. Would he relive discovering the body every time he went into that bathroom? Would Fabrizio? Would they ever be happy in their home again?

It had taken the sheriff's office a pretty long time to finally decide they needed to get to work on this case. Not a real confidence booster, even if they had finally put their top dog (which was what I considered Quincy) to work on it.

All of a sudden the urge to get back to the scene of the crime was fierce. Maybe the police had missed something the first time they'd checked it out. After all, they hadn't really been looking for evidence that anyone else had been there besides Elroy Villars. They could have missed a whole bunch of clues as to who killed Percy's brother.

Halfway across the lobby, I spun on my heel and turned toward the grand staircase, intent on finding Harry and getting the key to *la petite maison*.

"Melanie Hamilton? Wait. Stop."

Oh, crap. Was that who I thought it was?

"Hold up."

It was.

I stopped walking and turned, dreading the exchange about to take place, forcing a neutral look on my face, not quite able to manage a smile.

"Sydney." I kept my voice low and even.

She teetered up to me on leopard-print slides with what had to be four-and-a-half-inch stiletto heels. Her clothes looked expensive, some highfalutin designer outfit she'd wear when breezing in for a decaf soy latte at a trendy Palm Beach coffee shop. Her curly blonde locks were pulled back from her face. Her cheeks were pink, her eyes blue. She looked like a Barbie doll.

Could I even begin to compete with her? The doubt was alive for just the briefest of moments.

"Tattoos. That's what you do, right? Tattoos?" she chirped.

"Well, yes," I said slowly, wondering where this was going.

"Well, I need one. Can you do it?"

"Now?" I looked around. "You want me to ink now?"

She pressed her lips together and nodded.

"It's my day off," I said. "But on days I do work, appointments are made in advance. The resort prefers it that way."

She crossed her arms, cocked a hip, and pouted. "Jack said you'd do it. He said even if it was your day off you'd be glad to do it."

"He did?" That didn't sound like Jack. Even if this woman had wormed her way back into his heart, it wasn't like him to impose on another person.

My suspicion must have been showing because she opened her eyes really wide and tucked her chin.

Oh, yeah, sure. Like that ingénue act is gonna work with me? No way, sistah.

"Jack must have figured you'd do it for him." I was having some trouble deciding if what she was doing with one of her eyes was a wink or a tick. "I really need it before the costume ball. I'm going as a girl pirate, and I want Jack to see it."

She laid her hand on my arm, and it took just about all the self-control I could muster not to slap it away.

Several thoughts took a jog through my mind. This woman had either come here on her own after reconnecting with Jack in Florida, or she had been sent by Jack's mother for what appeared to be the sole purpose of stealing my Cap'n Jack away. Also, if the petite blonde interloper *was* telling the truth, Jack had sent her my way. And I could only come up with two reasons for that—either he was, in fact, sweet on her and wanted her to have the tattoo she had her heart set on, or he wanted her out of his hair for a while. I chose to believe it was that latter. To ride this out, I had to believe he was still in love with me. Lastly, it occurred to me that if I took the time to do her ink, I'd have her alone and maybe get a chance to figure out her strategy for hijacking my man.

Granddaddy Joe's slow drawl rolled through my brain with one of his infamous muddled idioms, "Keep your friends close-by, Mellie gal, and your enemies close-by too, like maybe tied up in the closet where you can check on them and make sure they ain't up to no good. " Lord, I missed my granddaddy.

I couldn't exactly put Sydney Baxter in a closet, but my stronghold, Dragons and Deities, would surely run a close second.

I smiled at Sydney, who'd surprisingly been waiting patiently for me to respond. Since I was on the wrong side of my smile, I could only hope it wasn't evil as Hannibal Lecter when I said, "Sure, Sydney. I'll give you a tattoo. Why the heck not?"

CHAPTER FIFTEEN

"What do you think of these?" I'd flipped the screen on my computer to the next page of fonts.

"Ooh, that's it." Sydney's manicured finger pointed to Edwardian Script, a particularly flowery scroll. "That's the one I want you to use for my tattoo."

Sydney had changed into one of the salon smocks Harry and I had chosen when we first set up the shop. They were gender specific and looked nearly medieval in design to go with the days-of-old theme of the tattoo parlor.

When I'd handed one to her, Sydney had said, "Are you sure this one's suitable for me. I have a twenty-inch waist, just like Scarlett O'Hara, you know."

I gritted my teeth. "Scarlett's waist was seventeen inches. If the smock doesn't fit, I'll find you one that does."

Sydney had emerged from behind the changing screen wearing the smock, a look of distaste puckering her face. Holding the fabric away from her, she'd asked, "Are you positively sure this thing has been to the laundry since your last customer used it?"

"Positively sure," I'd said brightly.

"I just hope to God that Jack doesn't decide to pop in and see how I'm doing. I'd rather die than have him see me in this ratty old thing."

I didn't respond but gestured toward the chair, not the cushy lie back and chill out chair but the crawl on and put your face in the hole chair. She wanted a small tattoo of scrolled initials just below her left shoulder. The initials were *J A S*, which (she'd made it a point to tell me five times already) stood for John Allen Stockton. Jack. My Jack. The woman was having my Jack's initials tattooed on her body. *Grr.* My fingers itched to ink something entirely different on her snowy shoulder, something inappropriate, something that would make a sailor blush. *Now, now, you're a professional, and she's a customer of the resort. Put on your big girl panties, and take one for the team.*

So, big girl panties on, I leaned over her, swabbed her skin with alcohol, and turned on the inking gun. *Breathe in. Breathe out. It's just a tattoo, like any other tattoo.* But it wasn't, and no telling myself it was would make it so.

"You know. I was happy to see you looking so much more presentable today than usual." Her words were partially smothered by the ring of cushion around her face, but I, like a dentist, had enough practice at translating a person whose mouth was inhibited, so I understood her perfectly.

More presentable? What? "I'm sorry?"

"Well, that thing you had on yesterday was just horrible," she said.

"Oh." She must have seen me in my work costume yesterday.

"It was so, so…dowdy."

Your mother should have told you to never say "dowdy" to a woman with an ink gun in her hand.

But I bit my cheek to keep from screaming and merely said, "It's my work costume." Mentally adding *Twit!* and *Jack thinks it's sexy in an Elvira Mistress of the Dark sort of way.*

I leaned over her milky soft skin and aimed my ink gun, thinking a stun gun would have been great to have right about then.

The tiny little tattoo, just the initials and a few curlicues and flourishes here and there, nothing at all elaborate or challenging—shouldn't have taken very long.

—but—

Because Sydney kept breaking out into bouts of crying—no, not just crying, wailing—and panting, like she was in labor or something—we had to stop the process every few minutes so she could gather herself.

At one point she looked at me, eyes red-rimmed and swollen, nose runny, and whispered, "A woman in love will put herself through hell to please her man."

When we were finally done and she'd composed herself, she asked to see it. Before bandaging it, I gave her the hand mirror and spun her around to see the reflection of her back in the large mirror on the wall.

"Mmm. It's very nice." She said, sounding surprised. "You really are as talented as Jack said you are." Then she seemed to realize she might have said something decidedly uncatty to me and pushed herself up off the chair. "I'll just change out of this, this thing and be on my way."

While she went back behind the changing screen, I ran her credit card.

When Sydney came back around the screen, I went over the aftercare instructions with her and gave her the kit that consisted of an instruction sheet, antibacterial soap, and special ointment to use on the tattoo.

"It'll begin to peel in about three to seven days," I finished. "When it does, discontinue the ointment and keep it dry until—"

"So it only lasts three to seven days? Well, that should be okay. The costume ball is tomorrow night. I only need it for that long. You know, to show off to Jack."

Oookay. "Sydney." I wasn't quite sure how to begin. "In three to seven days, it will begin to peel, like a sunburn. But after the peel, the art will still be on your skin."

"So, what do I need to do to get it off?" She looked down at the bag in her hand. "Just use this soap to scrub it?"

"Uh. No."

"Then what?"

"It won't come off. If you decide you don't want it, you'll need to have it removed by a professional. "

She looked at me for a moment then laughed. "No. You're just shining me on. Right? I mean I see little kids wash them off all the time. And actors in movies get temporary tattoos, don't they?"

I shook my head. "Those aren't real tattoos."

She twisted around and glanced back at the bandage, which was now under her knit top. "And this is…?"

"Permanent."

She flinched at the word. "But I don't want… I didn't think… Nobody ever told me." She glared at me. "If you think I'm not stopping the payment for paying for this, you'd better think again. And you can bet I'll be talking to the manager."

"But Jack already knows these aren't fake tattoos." I couldn't believe how calm my voice was.

"I…I…well, crap." Her mouth drew into a bitter, tight line. "We'll just see about this." She turned abruptly and headed for the door.

I watched her go, hoping for her sake when her wedding night came she would have wound up with someone whose initials are J A S because John Allen Stockton, alias Cap'n Jack, wouldn't be the man who took her on a honeymoon.

I wasn't going to take a passive role in this triangle, not for even one more minute. I'd given Jack time to take care of this, a whole day and half, as well as space, took a room in the resort, and he hadn't been successful. I folded my arms and made a mental inventory of what I had in my war chest and prepared myself for battle, just like Jean Lafitte.

Not more than ten minutes after Sydney had stormed out, Catalina Gabor, all aglow and excited, waltzed into Dragons and Deities. She carried a big, cream-colored shopping bag with the words *Brenda's Bridals* scrolled on it in silver letters.

I was still cleaning my equipment after having worked on Sydney.

"Hmm," Cat said. "I thought you were off today."

"So did I. Sydney Baxter had something else in mind." I regaled the tail of Sydney's inking session.

Cat sat with her hand over her mouth, and I could tell she was trying not to laugh. When I came to the part about the tattoo washing off, she lost the battle and snorted. Her total lack of self-consciousness was one of the things I loved about her. Cat was Cat, take it or leave it.

"Don't laugh," I said. "I almost feel sorry for her."

Cat sobered and wagged a finger at me. "Huh-uh. No feeling sorry for the enemy. You've got to be ruthless, merciless, serious. She's after your man, Mel. You can't have even the smallest soft moment."

I didn't know what to say, so I changed directions. "What's in the bag?"

It worked. She took the bait and switched subjects. "Only the most yummy fabrics the seamstress gave me to look at for the wedding. Wait'll you see."

And with that she began pulling samples of fabric from the bag, each more beautiful than the one before it. And when they were all spread out across the chaise in the corner of my studio, we put our heads together over them, pulling one after the other.

"This one for you," she said, snatching up a swatch of teal silk.

"Or this one?" I reached for a swatch of royal purple charmeuse that pooled softly in my hand.

"Oh, yes, that is lovely," Cat said.

We spent a few more minutes looking at all the fabrics and notions she'd brought, pairing the cream silk with those seeded pearls, that gorgeous purple charmeuse with color-matched chiffon for the sleeves and bodice. Then we put everything back in the bag from the bridal shop.

I stood up beside her as she picked up the bag. "I'm so happy for you and Quincy," I said and hugged her.

"Stop it." She sniffed. "You'll make me cry, and my mascara will run."

Something I'd thought of earlier popped back into my head. "Off the subject, do you have time to schedule a free reading for Nancy Villars?"

She shrugged. "The sister of the man who was killed?"

I nodded.

"I could make that work. What do you have in mind?"

"I talked to her earlier today. I don't know that she actually lied to me, but I didn't feel like she told me everything she could have. I'm willing to bet there're things going on with Nancy and with Percy that relate in some way to what happened to their brother—things that they're both leaving out."

"Sure," Cat said. "I'll call her room, tell her she won a free reading, and give her a couple of times today she could come to the House of Cards and have it done."

I hugged her again. "You're the best. I know snooping around behind your boyfriend's back isn't like you, and you aren't even the one who'd said she'd check into the Villars background and Elroy's death. That was me. I really appreciate—"

She cut me off. "Oh, stop it. You know I love fumbling around in people's closets to bring out all their skeletons just as much as you do."

We both turned at the sound of a voice clearing, and my heart swelled at the sight of Jack Stockton standing in the open doorway, in one hand a bouquet of peachy peonies and in the other the unmistakable cream-colored, pink-ribboned gift bag from Hové Parfumeur Ltd., which, if I had my guess, was soap or lotion or perfume of their Pirate's Gold scent that both Jack and I loved.

Cat's eyes went straight to the bag, and she laid her hand on my arm in a would-you-look-at-that way.

"Hi, Jack," Cat said when she saw my emotion had rendered me mute.

Jack said, "Hey, Cat. How're you doing?" But his eyes never left mine. "Mel." The subtext was full of longing.

"Jack." So much was behind that one word from me— need, love, hurt, yearning, regret. I was too full of emotion, and I couldn't have said more if I wanted to, which I didn't.

I only wanted to stand there and look at him—look at his long, strong body, dark, wavy hair, luscious full lips, and the sexy five o'clock shadow that never seemed to go away whether it was five o'clock or not. And I loved his eyes, eyes as warm and liquid as brandy and at the moment full of pleading.

I wanted to run to him and throw myself into his arms, but pride, even though I knew how stupid it was, stopped me.

In my side-vision Cat looked from me to Jack then back to me. "I should leave," she said awkwardly.

What do you think about that? So much is bubbling beneath the surface here, it's too intense for even the never-at-a-loss Catalina Gabor.

Jack suddenly snapped out of it. "No," he said, gesturing at the swaths of fabric on the chaise. "You ladies are doing something important here. I just wanted to bring these to you, Mel. To tell you I'm sorry I've hurt you, that I love you and miss you. I've sent for my mother. She'll be here later today. While she's here, I'll be setting things straight with her one way or another." His gaze held mine, and I felt tears start behind my eyes. "And I'm working on the other thing, too. You can count on it."

He stepped through the door into the suite, and while I looked up into his wonderful face, willing him to lower his head and press his lips against mine, he leaned over and whispered in my ear. "I love you. And I miss you, baby. I want you back in my house, in my bed. I can't take knowing you're hurt and upset. I'm going to fix it. I promise."

Tears filled my eyes, and the feelings were so strong I even sobbed.

He reached down and lifted one of my hands, laid the peonies in the crook of my elbow, and draped the handle of the gift bag across my palm. Another whisper. "Just a little something for you to model for me the next time we're alone." He kissed my cheek, turned, and walked away, leaving me standing there crying and laughing and breathing hard.

"Holy Moses," Cat said.

I turned and looked at her. In all honesty I'd forgotten she was there.

"Hot. Louisiana pepper sauce hot." She fanned herself. "But in the end, he's just a man, and that conniving blonde is a pretty little thing. She might not hold a candle to you, but we're gonna take some steps to make sure he knows that. There can't be any room for doubt in that man's mind that you're the best woman in the world and you were meant to be together. No mama. No Sydney. Just you and him."

I didn't answer, thinking about the fragrance in the gift bag and that Jack had said he wanted me to model it for him, and I couldn't help but smile at the thought—just the fragrance, nothing else?

CHAPTER SIXTEEN

Cat had to hurry back to the House of Cards for a scheduled tarot card reading. Since it was technically still my day off, I had an afternoon project in mind that had nothing to do with body art.

After what Nancy had said about her brothers always—and she'd reiterated *always*—being together, I felt as though I needed to get into Harry's house, to be where the killing had actually taken place.

If Percy had lied about not breaking into Harry's place with Elroy, if Percy and Elroy had fought and then Percy had killed Elroy, I needed to know, and I needed to know now. For the sake of Harry Villars. Percy Villars had put himself close to Harry, Harry my friend, and I had no intention of standing by and letting anything happen to my sweet employer, his resort, or the jobs of all my friends.

Before I did anything else in relation to Elroy's murder, I wanted to eliminate Percy from my list of suspects and make sure Harry wasn't in imminent danger being around him. It was hard to imagine that someone could have—how had Quincy put it?—"bludgeoned to death" his twin, his other half, but anything was possible when a lot of money was involved.

Because the discovery of Elroy's body had been such a shock and had rendered me so stunned, I'd not paid a lot of attention to my surroundings. I wanted a chance to look at the crime scene again anyway. Toward that end, I called Fabrizio and asked him to meet me at the employee's side entrance of the main building.

"Of course, m'dear," Fabrizio said, sounding a little out of breath. "I'm just finishing here at the gym. I've been engaged by the documentary film crew to enact a séance tonight on behalf of the Powells, dredging up the buccaneer Lafitte. Decided to hit the gym to be in prime shape for the performance. They'll be filming, and you know how this old thespian does love a juicy role. I'm just ready to step into the shower. Might you be amenable to waiting, oh, say fifteen or twenty minutes?"

"Yes," I said, "I might at that," not voicing the thought that I could definitely wait if I detoured through the main kitchen to see what Chef Valentine Cantrell had on the stove.

Sunday's heavy meal at The Mansion at Mystic Isle was always an old-fashioned dinner served in the main dining room between twelve thirty and two thirty in the afternoon in the Southern Sunday-after-church tradition. Sunday evening supper was more casual, and I could smell the red beans and ham hocks, the chicken pot pies, and shrimp gumbo she'd be serving later before I was anywhere near the kitchen.

Valentine Cantrell was, in the minds of most denizens of Louisiana, the female counterpart to Emeril Lagasse. She knew Southern food better than she knew her own face in the mirror. The woman could cook, which was how I found her then, standing in front of the enormous stove over the gumbo pot, talking to one of the kitchen workers.

She turned around as I walked through the door into the enormous stainless steel-clad kitchen. "Well, would you lookee what the cat done dragged in." She moved over and reached around me, hugging but careful not to touch me with her hands. "It's good to see you. Did you come to see your girl, Valentine, or did you come to eat?"

"Bit of both?" I said, raising my eyebrows in question.

She laughed, a hearty, full sound that started somewhere in Valentine's core and worked its way out. "More of one than the other, I'm thinking," she said. "What's your pleasure, Miss Melanie?" Before I could open my mouth, she went on. "Gotta be the red beans. Right? And a dab o' rice?"

I grinned.

"I knew it," she said, laughing again. "You're just an open book, child."

I sat at one of the long tables in the enormous kitchen and chowed down on the iconic Louisiana dish made even more mouthwatering by Valentine's secret herbs and spices—Colonel Sanders had nothing on Chef Valentine Cantrell—as she brought me up to date on what was happening with her and her adorable, brilliant son, Benjy. After what had happened at Christmastime, I was so glad to see things were back to normal with them.

After a while, she switched subjects. "I been hearing talk goin' round that some long lost wannabe relatives of Mr. Villars turned up, and one of 'em got hisself killed over at *la petite maison*. I'm willing to lay money you know something 'bout that."

I took a long, deep drink of sweet tea before wiping my mouth and sitting back. "Thanks for feeding me, Valentine. Delish as usual." I sighed. "So, yes, the rumor mill is just about as accurate as it can get. I spoke to Quincy Boudreaux earlier today, and the cause of death's got the sheriff's office investigating this mess as a homicide."

She'd sat down across from me, nursing a cup of what smelled like chicory and coffee. After listening with some intensity, she nodded slowly when I finished, her golden eyes knowing and sad, her full lips pinched. "The minute I heard there was some crazy kind o' papers round here what belonged to that scoundrel Lafitte, I knew it would bring us nothing but bad luck and trouble." She paused before wrapping both hands around her coffee cup and leaning toward me to reinforce her statement. "I want you to watch yourself, sweet child. I've seen how you get yourself all caught up in these terrible things. And while God knows you're good at coming up with answers, when something like this happens, seems like there's always at least one someone who doesn't appreciate you asking the questions."

Her melodic voice had taken on a low and ominous tone, and I had to shake off a shiver. "I'm worried all this"—I waved my hand toward the frosted glass window where the blurry forms of thrill seekers and treasure hunters could be seen wandering the grounds—"commotion and press is bad for Mystic Isle."

She patted my hand. "You're a good girl, and I love you for it. Just take care."

I always do. I looked up at the big clock. It was time to meet Fabrizio. I thanked Valentine for the grub and the empathy and left the kitchen.

I'd only just sat at one of the patio dining sets on the covered terrace by the employee lounge and side entrance when Fabrizio came outside to join me.

The Sunday afternoon sunshine angled under the terrace overhang. Dark clouds looked to be building up over the cypress trees further out in the bayou, and the warm, humid day just might be turning cooler if the promise of rain came to fruition. But for now the temp in the low eighties along with the total lack of any breeze made for a stifling atmosphere on the employee terrace.

Fabrizio sat quietly with me, fanning himself with a copy of *Where Y'At*, the issue from several months earlier with The Mansion on the cover. "My boy's been quite pensive since Deputy Boudreaux delivered the shocking assessment," he said in answer to my question as to how Harry had taken the news that the sheriff was proceeding with a homicide investigation. "This whole matter has him quite disturbed."

"I get it," I said. "The murder is why I asked you to meet me. Before the police get to crawling all over the house again, I was hoping you could give me a key so I could have another look at the place on my own."

"Key?" He looked at me. "To *la petite maison*?"

I nodded.

"Oh," he said thoughtfully. "I imagine that might well be arranged." He reached into the pocket of his lightweight sweat pants and pulled out a key ring. "I even imagine you might persuade a certain older friend to go along and do a bit of sleuthing with you."

I couldn't help smiling. "But I thought a certain older friend had a séance to perform."

"Oh, yes, he does. But it isn't for several hours yet."

I stared at him. "Are you sure you want to go back there? I don't imagine they've, uh, cleaned the place up yet—since they're still investigating and all."

"Oh. You don't imagine the, uh, remains are still there?"

"Oh God, no," I said quickly. "But there will definitely be signs in some spots—maybe even quite a lot of signs—of the murder."

At that, Fabrizio's can-do attitude seemed to flag, but only a little. "I don't want you to face that terrible abode on your own. One never knows what danger might lurk at a scene of such violence." He stood and tugged down the sleeves of his T-shirt before thrusting back his thin shoulders in a military stance. "Here I stand, m'lady, your champion. At the ready to do battle on your behalf."

I took hold of his hand and patted it. "Well," I said. "I don't think it will come to that."

His posture sagged. "Oh, thank God."

CHAPTER SEVENTEEN

———

Fabrizio and I hoofed it over to the employee parking lot where we hopped into his beat-up 1976 Volkswagen Beetle, the one he'd bought to drive to Louisiana several years ago. After immigrating to the US from England and landing in New York full of hope for a renewed career in theater *across the pond*, a career that never materialized, Fabrizio had answered an internet ad for "a distinguished actor capable of a convincing portrayal of a spirit medium."

The drive had taken Fabrizio over two weeks because he'd had to stop at several places along the route to hustle up work to pay for gas and repairs to the ancient VW. But it got him here, and when he'd finally made it to Mystic Isle near the lush Barataria Preserve in southeastern Louisiana near the Mississippi Delta, home to—guess who—Jean Lafitte, he'd found a newly renovated Southern plantation being repurposed as a unique resort dedicated to magic and the paranormal. Oh, and he'd also found the love of his life, none other than Harry Villars, his sweet and gentle yet funny and eccentric soul mate.

As we made our way over to *la petite maison*, the little VW Bug coughed and wheezed and bunny hopped until the engine warmed up. I'd quit asking Fabrizio why he didn't trade the poor thing off for something more dependable, maybe something that came off the line in this century, because it was just obvious he held a certain fondness for it. The car was so old, it was getting hard to tell what color it was. I thought maybe cream colored but couldn't be sure because of the thick patina.

Fabrizio pulled the car into the freestanding garage behind the house. While there was still crime scene tape on the front door, there was none across the French doors into the master bedroom at the side of the house, so Fabrizio unlocked those doors, and we went in.

The bedroom shutters were closed, making the room dark for threeish in the afternoon, even for October when the sun set a bit earlier than the month before. It was also eerily quiet. The whole house was tomb quiet, the silence broken only by the ticking of Harry's grandfather clock in the parlor. It made the sound of Fabrizio's whisper jarring. "I've never done this sort of thing before. If you don't mind, I'll follow your lead."

I didn't admit to him that I wasn't exactly the expert he seemed to think but just nodded as he fell into step behind me.

Either the room had been tossed, or Harry and Fabrizio weren't the neat freaks I'd figured them to be.

"Well, bloody hell," Fabrizio muttered from behind me.

I turned around to catch him picking up clothing that had been left in a pile on the floor.

"No." I said in a soft voice. "Don't touch anything, Fabrizio. They'll know we were here if you do too much housekeeping."

He stared at the pajama top he held in his hand before letting it drop back to the floor. "Sorry."

"No problem," I said. "Instead of tidying up, why don't you look for anything unusual or out of place, something that doesn't belong."

He tightened his lips and squinted in a decidedly Dirty Harry sort of way and nodded before doing an about-face and beginning what looked to be an all-out effort at scrutinizing the room.

I went the opposite direction he did, and we came back together at the door to the hallway.

"Anything?" I asked.

"I've just now noticed that the stand for the bog roll's gone missing."

"The what?"

"Right," he said. "Let me just translate that. In the loo there was a rather large antique wrought iron stand that held the roll of bathroom paper. It's no longer there."

Remembering what Quincy had said about Elroy having been hit with something heavy, I asked. "Do you think it could have been the murder weapon?"

Fabrizio shuddered visibly. "I don't know. I suppose."

"How terrible," I said.

He gulped and nodded.

I tried to shake it off. "Okay, moving on."

Our search of the house was methodical, slow, room to room. In the kitchen Fabrizio turned up a receipt from the resort gift shop he thought didn't belong to either him or Harry. "Anything we would get from the resort gift shop would go on an account. There wouldn't be an individual receipt."

We carefully tucked it into his wallet and then went on to the parlor where…

"What the heck is that?" Something small lying on the floor near the leg of the gorgeous leather sofa had caught my eye. I bent low to have a look at it then picked it up. "Huh," I said, turning it over in my hand before holding it up closer to my eyes.

It was a tie tack or lapel pin or something like that in an antique bronze metal. The letters *S P L A C* were stacked up against each other to form a curved shape. At one end of the pin was a smooth round shape with (what looked like) eyes etched into it.

Fabrizio had come up behind me and was peering over my shoulder.

"Something you recognize?" I asked.

"Not at all." It came without a second's hesitation. "What is it?"

I turned it over to show him the back. "A pin. There's something familiar about it, but I can't place it."

He scratched his head. "I can honestly say with a hundred percent confidence I've never seen that before."

"Do you think it might be Harry's or—"

Before he could answer, the sound of more than one vehicle pulling up outside the house interrupted me.

Fabrizio went to stand beside the front window and peered between the slats of the shutters. "Bloody marvelous, it's the sheriffs."

My heart leapt as a shot of pure adrenalin rushed through me. "Oh crap, Fabrizio. We gotta get outta here. It's against the law in this parish to cross a police line, and Quincy'll haul us off to the hoosegow f'sure."

He shook his head slowly, still peering out the window. "Nothing of the sort, m'dear. He's your friend."

"Like that matters to Quincy Boudreaux?" I was already moving back toward the bedroom. "He will. He's done it before. That's one man who doesn't like the general population messing around in his investigations. Now come on. Let's get out of here."

We hustled down the hall to the bedroom as quickly and quietly as possible, and I was just closing the French door behind me when I heard the front door open and several voices echo down the hall.

A finger to my lips, I indicated the lock. Fabrizio turned the key in it, and we headed back out to the garage and the antique Beetle. The garage sat far enough away from the house that we were able to back out of it, pull around to the back of it, and make our way back to the main resort without any of the deputies who'd arrived with Quincy being aware of our little recon mission.

It wasn't until we were well on our way back along the service road that I thought about the pin from the parlor. I opened my hand to have a closer look at it.

Fabrizio noticed me staring at it. "Are you going to share that and the receipt with the constables?"

I gaped at him. "You're kidding, right?"

"Oh," he seemed confounded at that. "I wasn't. No."

"If Quincy finds out I lifted what could turn out to be evidence from his crime scene, he'll have me drawn and quartered."

"Oh." Fabrizio cocked an eyebrow, his voice full of irony. "Are you sure? Drawn and quartered? That sounds just a touch severe."

CHAPTER EIGHTEEN

———

On the way back to the main building I received a text message from Cat.

Nancy Villars jumped at a free tarot reading and hustled right over to the House of Cards. Man, is she intense. Meet me in the main salon for a glass of wine. You're gonna love it.

So I thanked Fabrizio for going sleuthing with me and asked him to drop me off at the front entrance and also to please keep me posted on what he learned from checking up on the receipt he'd found at the house. From the veranda I went straight in and made the right turn into the main salon. Tired and stressed from such a bizarre day, I totally felt the funeral dirge ringing out as I crossed the entry seemed pretty darn appropriate.

The main salon was one of my favorite places in the resort. When the main building had been constructed for the Villars back in the 1700s, the huge front room had been designed to host parties the like of the barbecue at Twelve Oaks in *Gone with the Wind*. I'd never seen The Mansion before Harry restored it, but from what I'd heard, it was sad—the floor covered in ratty 50s-style turquoise and pink patterned carpet, with sheer, floor-length pink drapes at all the windows, left over from the Eisenhower years.

But the restoration had brought the salon floor back to its original hardwood, polished to a high sheen. It was covered here and there with lovely circular rugs where antebellum loveseats and high-backed chairs set off conversation areas. A bar in the gently curved pre-Civil War style sat centered at the back of the room. At four in the afternoon, the tinkling of "Raindrops Keep Falling on My Head" from Tatiana at the baby grand by the windows barely floated above the low buzz of conversation.

Tiny café tables clustered in small groups around the bar. Cat had commandeered one of them.

I made my way straight to the bar and ordered a glass of pinot grigio then carried it to the table. Cat looked up from her wine glass as I sat down.

"You look frazzled," she said. "Long day?"

I nodded and took a sip of the cool, fruity wine, snatched a Kalamata olive off the small plate of cheese, crostini, and cold cuts in the middle of the table.

Cat's gentle, welcoming smile, the chilled wine, and the soft music washed over me, and the stress of the day left like someone had pulled a thread, and my taut nerves had been unstrung.

"Yes," I said. "Long day." It had been, between my frenetic impersonation of Sue Grafton's intrepid PI, Kinsey Millhone, running here, there, and everywhere poking around in other people's business, and dealing with my nemesis, Sydney Baxter. And it wasn't over yet. I just needed a temporary escape to a place where I didn't have to worry about murderers or man-stealers.

I pulled the small plate on my side of the table closer and claimed some of the cheese, two small crusts of bread, and some shreds of pancetta. Cat seemed impatient to get my attention and reached out with splayed fingers. I looked back up at her face.

"So you want to hear about this, right?" Her eyes were bright, her features animated. "I can really see how a person gets addicted to this detective stuff. I actually got sort of a high from grilling Nancy Villars for details and trying to make sure she didn't know I was doing it."

The goat cheese practically melted in my mouth. I swallowed then dabbed the corners of my lips daintily, as if I hadn't just fallen on the food like a vampire at a blood bank. One of the cocktail waitresses came up and set a plate of oysters on ice, a bowl of lemon wedges, and several tiny bottles of Tabasco in between us.

"Oh my goodness gracious, girl," I said. "This is just perfect."

"I know." Cat smiled wickedly at me, and we both attacked the offerings.

Between slip-sliding the oysters, making mini-sandwiches of the bread, cheese, and pancetta, and sipping the wine, Cat unfurled the story of Nancy Villars' tarot card reading as if storytelling was her main occupation—which in a way, it was.

She cleared her throat and began. "Like I said in my text, Nancy almost came running for her free reading, plopped down in the client chair, and leaned over the table like she was expecting me to hand her a fistful of cash or something. I used a marked deck of course, so even after she cut them, the cards that I wanted to come up did."

"Aren't *all* your decks marked?"

She sniffed. "Of course not. Most of the time I let the cards fall where they may—so to speak. Just on occasion do I need to manipulate the client. The very rare occasion."

"Like this one."

"Yes, like this one. Now. Are you going to let me tell you this, or are you going to keep interrupting?"

"Sorry."

She settled back into it. "I had her draw three cards, and then I sat looking at them for a long time, pondering, doing my thing." She interlaced her fingers beneath her chin and batted her lashes. "I figured I might as well give her the whole treatment, you know. First I looked at the Three of Swords."

I could see it in my mind. The Three of Swords was a particularly dramatic card depicting a beautiful red heart cruelly pierced by three shining swords.

"I looked up at her and asked her if she was sad," Cat said. "That the card can indicate sadness or a difficult time in a relationship. So then she tells me that yes, she *has* been sad."

"Well, yeah, we know that much already. Her brother was murdered. Of course, she's—"

"No." She interrupted me. "That wasn't why she said she was sad. She went on and on about this man she'd been seeing for the last year. This guy was a real doozey, Mel. Not only did he love her and leave her, but before he took off, he drained her of just about every nickel she'd ever saved."

"What a prince."

"Yeah."

I leaned forward over the table, caught up in Cat's story of how she'd led Nancy Villars down the primrose path, trying to get information from her. "So she brought up this tragic love affair before she mentioned how sad she was at the loss of her brother?"

"That's just it." Cat threw up her hands. "She didn't mention the loss of her brother at all—not at first, anyway. Not in relation to her sadness. Said the source of all this wretchedness I was seeing in the cards—that's the word she used, *wretchedness*—was the loss of her one true love."

"Wretchedness? Her one true love? I don't know what to think about that."

"Oh. Wait, girlfriend. It gets better. I moved on then to the next card. I'd fixed things so Nancy would draw the King of Pentacles, and I could feel her out about her finances. And since Nancy had already admitted the swine took her and her assets for one heck of a ride, it made sense for me to act as if she might be looking at a reversal of fortunes, a financial opportunity on the horizon."

"And?"

"And, sister, did she ever jump on that. Began singing me a song about how she just knew something good was going to come from Elroy's death. About how she and her other brother can work together on some windfall project."

"So all she had to say about Elroy's murder was how it affected her? Nothing about being sad, how she'd miss him, or anything like that?" I was stunned to silence for a moment but took the opportunity to drain my wine glass before drawing a long breath.

Cat nodded.

"That's cold," I said. "If she thinks it was such a good thing her brother died and put her next to this book deal with Percy, it makes you wonder if she might not have helped it along. Nancy's a big, strong girl, and under the right conditions, I betcha she could put enough force behind *a blunt object*—as Quincy put it—to kill a man."

Cat just stared at me before shivering visibly.

"Is that all you learned?" I asked. "I mean that's plenty..."

"That's not all, *chère*," she said softly. And I couldn't help but think that after spending so much time with Quincy Boudreaux, she might be turning into a little curvy, brunette version of the cocky Cajun. "Then I read the third card, The Hermit. That card can indicate a turnaround. I call it the fixer-upper card when it shows up in the right aspect. After what she'd said already, I asked her if she could imagine circumstances that would turn things around and make her happy again."

"And she said?"

"That with the death of her brother, maybe things had already been set in motion to fix her life—that finding the Lafitte document would validate her brother Percy's claim to the genuineness of Belle's story, and now that she'd be helping him with the book, they'd both be rich as Croesus when it hit the bestseller list, and the money would bring back her lover."

"Oh boy," I said. "So if she manages to get any loose change out of working with Percy on this book, she's gonna call up this guy and let him know about it? She ought to just write him a check and put it in the mail. Doesn't she have any pride at all?"

"It's obviously affected her. How could it not?" Cat said. "She was especially contemptuous about Percy's love life."

"What did she have to say about Percy?"

"Just that he was engaged to be married to his longtime girlfriend but just recently broke off the engagement with no explanation. Nancy says the poor girl was heartbroken and that Percy was tightlipped about the whole thing and basically told everyone his reasons for doing it were none of their business. Said, 'I don't talk about it. Percy reacts strangely if I do.'"

"Huh," was all I could think of to say.

We just sat there looking at each other for a while until Cat asked, "Did you and Fabrizio turn up anything over at Harry's place?"

"Fabrizio found a receipt he was going to follow up on, and I found this." I reached into my jeans pocket and pulled out the pin. Cat leaned across and peered at it. "Here." I started to hand it to her, but she shook her head.

"I've been with my wild Cajun long enough to know not to put my fingerprints on something that might turn out to be evidence."

"Oh," I said. *Duh.* "Right. What do you think it is?"

Cat stared at it a moment longer then pursed her lips and looked out over the main salon where the lighting had subtly changed over the last hour to a lower, dreamier level. I waited as she considered what the tiny object might mean.

"It's obviously a pin of some sort," Cat finally said, pulling my thoughts back to the small item in my palm. "Like the Shriners wear or the Elks. And there's something familiar about it—"

"I thought that too." I jumped in.

She went on. "But I can't place what it is. Why don't you show it to Q, ask him?"

"Not likely," I said. "I came across this at Quincy's crime scene when he wasn't there and I wasn't supposed to be. Your lawman wouldn't be all that receptive to the idea that I carried away what might be evidence in one of his exclusive investigations."

Cat pushed her chestnut hair behind one ear. "You got a point there. I know I've seen that or something like it before. I'll keep thinking about it. In the meantime, I have to run. Don't forget to go to wardrobe and pick up the costume I chose for you." She clicked her teeth and whistled. "It's got the wow factor. When Cap'n Jack Stockton sees you in it, he'll be so thunderstruck he won't even remember the blonde's name."

"Thunderstruck?" I gave my head a little shake. "I'm not so sure I should have let you pick out my costume."

Cat just laughed.

We divvied up the check, left money on the table, and made our way outside.

It was late Sunday afternoon, four days since Elroy Villars had been left to rot at *la petite maison*, two days since Jack and I had returned from Florida, and one day since Sydney Baxter had shown up and turned me into a pouty, jealous child, also one day since a body had been discovered at Harry and Fabrizio's home.

Murder at Mystic Isle.

I had a lot to think about.

Murder.

Quincy and the sheriff's office had begun to work on it, but they were late to the investigation. I felt I already had more details about the case than they did, but so far the only real suspects were Elroy's own brother and sister and the Powells, who wanted to serve billions, just like McDonald's. But they definitely weren't the only people with motive—motive being possession of the valuable historical document that everyone under the sun seemed to be obsessed with getting their hands on.

CHAPTER NINETEEN

———

I headed to the rear of the resort, specifically the behind-scenes area we called *wardrobe*. It was where all the employees' costumes were made and maintained. The resort policy was for two costumes or uniforms to be allotted to each employee along with normal maintenance and cleaning. Above and beyond normal wear and tear, any damages were our responsibility. It was a fair policy, one with incentive for us to take care of the clothing provided so we wouldn't wind up paying for mending, extra cleaning, or even a whole new costume.

The wardrobe area was like a boutique on steroids. Everything from kitchen and housekeeping uniforms to costumes for the front desk clerks, all the way to the more elaborate getups like Fabrizio's monochromatic Nehru suits and turbans, Cat's gypsy soothsayer flowing skirts and peasant blouses, and my own dark vampiress gowns hung on racks throughout the area adjacent to the employee locker room. Keeping the apparel in shape for day-to-day work shift use as well as special occasions such as Mardi Gras, holidays, and other events was just about a 24/7/365 operation, and someone was always working in the department—even on Sunday after five, especially since it was the day before the Halloween costume ball coming up. The wardrobe division was also responsible for preparing costumes to be rented out.

Monday night's ball was the first of four to be held at the resort during the month of October. Harry Villars did love a good party, and he kept The Mansion's special events coordinator hopping with ideas for happenings connected with holidays or the resort's magic and supernatural themes in general. Harry had always said Halloween was one of his favorite celebrations, and it was observed at the resort the entire month of October. The masquerade balls were generally geared toward resort guests, but tomorrow's was open to employees as well.

Sugar Marchand, the hotel's head seamstress, was inside the cavernous room hunched over a sewing machine. She was working on a bright green Kermit the Frog costume.

She looked up when I walked in. Sugar was in her mid to late sixties and was pretty dang skinny, so much so my plump Grandmama Ida would have said Sugar was a woman in desperate need of a cheeseburger. Her face bore evidence of the thirty-nine years she admitted to having smoked two packs a day. Having quit years ago, these days a full-blown campaign against cigarette smoking and its evils was the zealous pulpit from which she preached. But the years of tobacco abuse had rendered her face like cracked leather. Sugar's hair was the rich color of a good merlot and cut really short.

"Miss Melanie Hamilton," she said, smiling and creasing her face even more.

"Sugar," I said. "What's shaking loose over here in wardrobe?"

Sugar stood and crossed to a rack where she took down a dark zipper bag. "Here you go, Madam Tattooist." She unzipped the bag. "This is what the doctor, well, what Miss Cat ordered for you. I used the measurements in your costume file to alter it. Should fit you like a glove."

She pulled back the flap revealing a short dress with a brown and white ruffled skirt and a bodice that was part vest, part lace-up blouse. "Ta-da," she crowed. "Pirate wench." Laying it aside, Sugar reached to an overhead shelf and brought down a box which she set on her worktable. "These go with it."

Inside the box was a pair of tall black boots with heavy buckles, a thick black belt, a beat-up looking tricorn hat, and a thinner belt with a scabbard. A fake-jewel-encrusted plastic handle stuck out of the leather scabbard.

Sugar ran a hand through her hair, leaving it standing straight up. "Ironic, don't you think? I mean seeing as how it's all about this Jean Lafitte thing these days. You'll be too cute for words tomorrow night. The costume's perfect for you. Think about adding some fishnet stockings, letting your hair go all wild and curly, and painting your lips all up with some Slut Red gloss. You'll be the bell of the ball."

I looked at the costume. It was pretty skimpy at both the hemline and the neckline, and God only knew I wasn't exactly a sexpot like a certain tarot card reader we all knew and loved. And while I wanted to look good enough to get Jack's attention, I certainly didn't want to show up at the masquerade ball looking desperate. "Maybe I should go for something less revealing," I said, looking doubtfully at Sugar.

She nodded and winked knowingly at me. "It reveals just enough. Trust me, girlfriend."

I had another look at the outfit. "Well," I said. "If you think so."

I zipped the bag, tucked the box under my arm, and took the hanger in my other hand. "Thanks for putting this aside for me, Sugar," I said.

"Oh, sure, honey. I couldn't find any more masks around here, but if you stop by the Masquerade Emporium, they'll have one for you."

As I went to the door, I couldn't help wondering if Sydney Baxter had plans to attend the costume ball, and if she did, what she'd be wearing.

Sugar sat back down in front of the sewing machine.

I left her to finish the Kermit costume as something else occurred to me. *It's not easy being green*—with envy that is, which is what I was and had been for the last couple of days. I didn't much like the way it made me feel.

I did stop at the Masquerade Emporium in the auxiliary wing of the resort. It was located beyond both Dragons and Deities and the House of Cards. The Emporium was where outfits for the costume balls were being rented to guests and where I picked up a shiny coppery half-mask that complimented the color of the pirate wench skirt and vest.

Who should I run into on my way out? Cat, Fabrizio, Chef Valentine Cantrell, Stella by Starlight, and Lurch, all heading in force into the costume rental store.

I was surprised to see them all together. "Guys," I said. "What's up?"

"Why, nothing," Fabrizio said quickly. "Why should anything be up? Anything at all?"

"Can't talk right now," Cat said, not even slowing down. "Running late, and I gotta get down to the ferry and head home."

Lurch made that low moaning sound I'd come to know was his way of saying: *Y'at? S'up?* Or *lez partay*. But the gentle giant wasn't looking at me when he moaned it, and after my gaze shifted between them, I realized none of them were. Instead they were all looking back and forth at each other—nervously.

Huh. What's up with that? But I didn't stop to find out, writing it off as probably having to do with the masquerade ball to be held tomorrow night. They were all probably just picking up their costumes or masks or something and wanted to be done before the store closed.

Cat had said she'd be leaving the resort to take The Mansion at Mystic Isle ferry back across the river to our apartment in the city. It had only been a few weeks that Cat and Quincy had been planning their wedding and monopolizing the cute little courtyard domicile on Dumaine Street in the heart of *le Vieux Carré* that Cat and I shared. And if I were being honest, up until last night when I'd slept alone in my hotel room without the warm body of Jack Stockton as big spoon to my smaller spoon, I hadn't minded being temporarily displaced from my own place—but tonight I was feeling a little homesick.

I reached into my pocket for my phone and went to the resort website scheduling page for Dragons and Deities to check my Monday appointments. I didn't have anything that I knew about until eleven a.m. when a guest had signed on for one of the copyrighted stock Mystic Isle wizard designs. During my stint at The Mansion at Mystic Isle, I must have inked at least fifty of the way-cool Merlin look-alikes on various bodies. Since I knew the design so well, I figured the work would go smoothly and quickly. It was a good thing I'd checked. Sometime between the last time I'd looked at the schedule and now, Roger Goodwin, Mr. Hollywood himself, had booked a two-hour slot beginning at eight thirty a.m.

"Huh," I said out loud to myself. "Wonder what kind of tattoo a movie director would ask for. This could be interesting."

It also could be a good opportunity for me to quiz him about his clients, the ultra-ambitious, highly-motivated Powells. But how to engage him? I didn't know all that much about Roger Goodwin movies, just a few scant details.

The sudden thought that popped into my head might have been courtesy of my Granddaddy Joe, or it might have just been a good old-fashioned excuse. Whatever. It didn't make any difference where it came from, I thought it was a brilliant idea for several reasons and decided I'd just jump right on it.

I backed out of the internet and dialed Jack's cell.

"Mel?" He spoke softly, his voice sounding surprised and a little confused. "Is something wrong?"

"Nothing's wrong," I said, feeling suddenly nervous. "Do you have any plans for tonight?" I waited, holding my breath.

"Uh"—he sounded nervous too—"no."

"Would you mind terribly if I came over to your place later to watch a few Roger Goodwin movies on Netflix?"

Again, holding my breath.

"Mind? Of course I don't mind. How can you even think that? I spent most of the day in my office trying to avoid…well, just working. Sure. Come on over." His voice softened. "Please. I need to see your face."

Not any more than I needed to see him, but I couldn't bring myself to say it. I pulled the phone from my ear and checked the time, five forty-five. Was an hour enough time to whip myself into a girly state so mouthwatering and desirable the man I loved wouldn't be able to even think about another woman? *Make it work, Mel. You don't want to keep him waiting.* "I'll be there at seven."

Back in my room, I steamed, I powdered, I lotioned, I fussed over my hair and just the perfect amount of makeup. I went to my suitcase (still packed and sitting in a corner as if it were expecting to be carried back to Jack's place) and pulled out my favorite teal sweater and best black jeans—the ones I had to lie on the bed to zip. With only a dab or two of the Pirate's Gold perfume Jack had given me behind my ears and between my breasts, I ensured he'd want to sit close to me (and maybe even let me *model* it for him).

I really did intend to watch whatever Roger Goodwin films we could find on Netflix, but surely it wouldn't hurt to look nice and smell great while I was at it.

Jack answered the door before I even knocked, and we stood there staring at each other for one breathless moment before he yanked me into his arms and laid a kiss on me that I swore lifted me a foot off the ground.

I had almost forgotten I was supposed to be upset with him, but it inconveniently popped back into my brain, and I somehow found the wherewithal to reluctantly pull away.

He was breathing hard, and his eyes had grown so dark, I couldn't help but think of Edward Cullen when he needed to feed. *Oh, baby, bite my neck.* It was only the drive to maintain at least some semblance of dignity that kept me from jumping his bones right there in the doorway. I really had missed him. What had I been thinking to avoid him?

"Come in," said the wolf to the lamb. His voice was husky.

The lamb couldn't help but think the wolf was so delish she might convert to carnivore or even predator. *Jack.* But that wasn't why I'd come tonight.

"I need to familiarize myself with Roger Goodwin's work so I'll have a conversation starter tomorrow morning when I talk to him about his clients, the Powells."

He cleared his throat then asked, "You have reason to believe it was one of the Powells who killed Elroy Villars?"

I lifted a shoulder. "I haven't ruled it out."

"Well"—he sounded resigned—"I looked up a couple of movies already, so I guess we better get to it."

He led me into the main room where the flat screen was already turned on and displaying the Netflix logo page. On the sleek glass and stainless steel coffee table in front of the leather sofa, a veritable junk food feast had been set up: cheddar cheese popcorn, Reese's Pieces, Milk Duds, an ice bucket, and several cans of Diet Dr. Pepper. All my favorites.

My stone-cold heart melted, and I turned to him. "Aw, Jack. You remembered."

He smiled. "Haven't you figured that part out yet, Mel? I remember everything about you. Every. Little. Thing."

My heart turned over, and I couldn't find my voice. How could I resist this man? How could I stay mad at him, especially when I didn't even want to. I forced my traitorous mind to focus on everything good about him, about us, about the way we were together. I didn't want to ruin this evening.

I moved to the sofa, fluffed up the throw pillow, sat down, and patted the empty spot beside me.

In no time at all, we were cuddled up and watching Goodwin's first big-money Indiana Jones-style flop, *Pharaoh's Ghost* (really awful) then when it was over (thank God), a better but somewhat type B sci-fi adventure he'd directed in the mid-80s, *Milky Way Mission* (which sent me diving for the Milk Duds). It felt so good, so normal to be next to Jack—it felt like home.

We were only about halfway through the second one—just as the crew at mission control lost contact with the spaceship—when someone knocked at Jack's front door.

I sat up, feeling the physical isolation of leaving the warm spot where I'd been leaning against his side. "Are you expecting someone?"

He stood. "No. I'm not."

When he opened the door and I heard the high-pitched, "Hey, sugar man, look what I brought," my reaction was so visceral it made me queasy—or maybe it was all the junk food, but I didn't think so.

Jack stepped into the open doorway, and it looked as if he might be trying to keep her from coming in, but it didn't work.

Sydney Baxter exploded into the main room like a tiny blonde Tasmanian devil, in one hand a bottle of wine and in the other a clear box of what appeared to be chocolate-covered strawberries from the resort sweet shop. "We can get drunk, feed these to each other, and see if maybe all our clothes don't just mysteriously fall off. I have something brand new to show you." She laughed but stopped cold when she saw me sitting on the couch. "Well, what the hell's *she* doing here?"

Good old Sydney. If someone ever needed to know how to spoil a perfectly nice evening, she'd be the person to ask. I wished she'd just leave, and as if Jack had read my mind…

Jack began. "Sydney, you should go back to the resort." Resort? I'd been thinking someplace farther, maybe Siberia. He went on. "Mel and I are in the middle of something here."

"Oh, sure. Work, I suppose. Well, that's all right if it's work." There was shrill hope in her voice.

"No. Not work," he said. Then more slowly, "Well, not exactly. We were just—"

"No problemo, sugar pants." She flounced over to the sofa and sat down next to me in the spot still warm from Jack. "I'll be quiet as a mouse so you can get your work done. You won't even know I'm here."

I just sat there a few beats, looking at her. Was it possible anyone could be that dense? I finally understood what Jack was dealing with—someone as dumb as a box of rocks who didn't get the message. Short of picking her up and throwing her out, he wasn't going to get rid of her. I stood. "I think I'll call it a night, Jack. Let me know when the two of you work this out." I picked up the box of Milk Duds and then, as an afterthought, the Reese's Pieces.

"I'll just let myself out."

As the door closed behind me, I could have sworn I heard Sydney squeal, "Oh goodness gracious, Jack. Is that *Milky Way Mission*? I just love, love, love that movie!"

CHAPTER TWENTY

———

Jack had come to the door and called after me. "Mel? Don't go." But the tone of his voice told me he really meant, "Don't leave me alone here with her." He'd sounded so frustrated that for a moment I thought about going back. But Miss Sydney was his problem to deal with. It was only fair he solve it.

And besides, I had felt like if I didn't get the heck outta Dodge, I'd wind up being sorry for one of two things: either saying something so cruel to her that I'd regret it the instant the words were out or maybe even socking Miss Sydney Baxter square in the nose.

I really couldn't blame the woman for giving it her best shot. Who wouldn't want that man back? Served her right for letting him go to begin with.

The walk from Jack's cottage to the main resort normally took twelve minutes. With adrenaline fueling my engine, I turned it into nine. It was almost ten o'clock.

Just as it was getting ready to close, I stopped by the Abracadabra coffee kiosk at the entry to the auxiliary wing, picked up a *cafe au lait* with double sugar, and carried it upstairs to my room. There were a few things I wanted to accomplish before I crashed (and what with the day I'd had, there was no doubt I would), so caffeine and sugar seemed like a good idea.

I'd been too tired to put things away when they'd brought them over from Jack's the night before, and now, standing in the middle of the lovely little junior suite and seeing my two bags just sitting there made me lonely for Jack. I had to wonder if Sydney would ever leave.

Ever, Mel? She's only been here two days. But it seemed like a millennium since I'd slept in Jack's warm arms.

I had to ask myself if there was a way to help Jack with the fluffy little piece of baggage and send her packing—a way to do it without breaking the law. Granddaddy Joe's old Remington shotgun stood waiting in my closet at Cat's and my apartment. But I was pretty sure kind-hearted Jack would rather Sydney be dealt with in a less violent manner.

Both Grandmama Ida and my mama, Della, were strong women who'd run their own lives and dealt with their own problems. From watching them, I'd learned that the hard part of being strong is standing back and trusting the ones they loved to sort things out for themselves—all the while, of course, propping them up with bushels of love and encouragement. Jack and I were meant to be equals in life. He wasn't my child or my prodigy. And as hard as this was, I had confidence if there was any way to let Sydney down easy, he'd find it.

I took a hot shower which cleared my head and calmed my impatience some. My thoughts were back on the case as I slipped on my sleep shirt and climbed up into the tall four-poster bed. With my laptop propped against my knees, I lay back on the pillow stack.

I'd talked to just about everyone I thought might be involved in the murder and still didn't have a real feeling for any of them, so my idea was to get to know them better. How? By stalking them on Facebook and Twitter, of course.

First I had a look at the Powells. They were practically omnipresent with both Theresa and Archie having their own personal pages, a couples page, and a professional page for their antiquity parlor in Boston. And that was just Facebook. They had similar coverage on Twitter, Pinterest, and Instagram. Even Wikipedia and a full-blown, ten-page website. By the time I was done checking them out, my head was spinning.

Theresa Powell, née Theresa Jackson, was a small-town girl with big-town ambitions. She listed her hometown as Macomb, Illinois, and it looked like once she was done with high school she'd left there and never looked back. Apparently having made a beeline to Chicago, she worked in an archeological museum as a tour guide. It was where she'd met Archie. He'd already been a semifamous adventurer with a "degree in archeology and a passion for adventure," which was a tagline I was pretty sure he'd pilfered from a TV adventure star. Theresa married him, and the two went back to Boston where she seemed to be the driving force behind their expansion and mutual quest to become a real-life Indiana Jones and Lara Croft.

I scrolled through dozens of photos of Theresa—in tight tank tops, cargo short-shorts, and climbing boots, her hair pulled back in one long braid and swung around over one breast, sexy smudges of dirt on her cheeks and nose—hard at work at some remote dig, I supposed.

After I finished checking out Theresa, I looked through an equally massive amount of posts and photos from Archie. Where her pages had been a narcissistic "look at me" log, his were mostly boasts of "look at her" tributes to his beautiful wife.

As I'd originally thought, Theresa was mostly after fame and fortune. But at second glance, I felt as if I'd misjudged Archie. While he postured for the cameras and said all the right things about seeking historical truths, thus expanding his and his wife's outreach and influence in the world of archeology, his true motivation seemed to be keeping the little woman happy. Happy wife—happy life? Based on their TV appearances and prolific media coverage promoting their various expeditions to the farthest reaches of the globe, all with Theresa Powell being the main focus, Archie apparently adored his younger, more ambitious wife and seemed set on doing everything in his power to make her the media star she longed to be.

Nancy Villars didn't have Pinterest or Twitter or Instagram, but I did find her on Facebook. Even though Cat's tarot card reading had revealed a great deal about her love life lost, her Facebook was a dead giveaway as to how devastating it had been when her lover left her.

Before she became the dumpee, Nancy had almost been a FB fanatic. Hanging out online, posting photos and videos day and night. She and the man went to the movies, to dinner, and on long (and what appeared to be expensive) weekend getaways. Unfortunately by looking at her social media page, a person could almost name the place, day, and hour the man had walked away. A professional photo of the couple at a dinner cruise on Lake Michigan revealed a dressed-up Nancy clinging to the arm of the bored-looking younger stud who happened to be checking his watch when the shutter snapped.

That had been a little over eight months ago, and Nancy hadn't posted a single word, photo, or video on her page since then. It was as if, at least according to Facebook, she'd stopped living. I thought of Belle Villars and her desperate expectations that Lafitte's letter of pardon would bring her lover back to her. Nancy Villars had pinned her hopes on the same fragile theory.

Percy and Elroy Villars had maintained separate pages. Both were quite active on both Facebook and Twitter, posting excited updates about their recent discovery of Belle's journal and how the secrets within it would take them on the greatest adventure of their lives.

Percy had entered his status as "in a relationship," although posts and other indications, as well as what his sister had told Cat, looked as if he'd broken off a formal engagement from his longtime girlfriend just weeks before the twins had come to Louisiana. Maybe he just hadn't gotten around to changing his status yet. Besides the stiff photos of Percy and his lady, a few carefully posed shots of him and Nancy and their parents, and the frequent news about the Lafitte connection, there was little content on his page.

Elroy, on the other hand, seemed to have been a more gregarious creature. His page was loaded with group pictures of Elroy and friends raising a few at sporting events and bars, pictures of Elroy and different good-looking women at night clubs, even pictures of Elroy, Percy, and Percy's pleasant-looking girlfriend at different places. There were no photos of Nancy or their parents on Elroy's page.

Percy's fiancée was listed as Juliette Johnson. She was a "friend" of each twin. I went to her page and clicked through her photos. I stopped at one of her and Percy that had obviously been taken before the two of them broke up. They were in a booth at a restaurant, and the light wasn't great. Percy and his ladylove leaned into each other, lips locked—heck, I thought there might be tongues involved, her hands in his red hair, his on the back of her neck. He had his eyes open. Hers were closed. And there they sat, tagged and everything: Percy Villars and Juliette Johnson. It was different than the photos I'd seen on Percy's page, less posed and more like a slice of life. It was lovely. They made a nice couple. Too bad it hadn't worked out for them.

What would it be like to be a twin, or to be in love with a twin? Bizarre, that's what I thought. Kind of like having your identity all mixed up with someone else's and not really being an individual. I didn't think I'd like it either way. I wouldn't want to be a twin—I didn't feel as if I'd ever know if the things I did were because of who I was or because of who *we* were. And if Jack was a twin, heck, how would I ever know if the man I was cuddling with was Jack or his twin brother? Yikes.

My eyes had begun to droop, and I caught myself nodding off. I closed the laptop, too tired to do more than just lay it off to the side.

In the end, neither the caffeine nor the sugar helped. I dropped off to sleep with the lights still on and thoughts of multiple Jack Stocktons and my complete and utter confusion about which one was the real Cap'n Jack filling my head.

CHAPTER TWENTY-ONE

―――――

It was early when I woke. Five thirty a.m. After what I put together about my key suspects the night before, it seemed important to meet with Fabrizio before my day began and find out what he'd learned about the gift shop receipt he'd discovered at *la petite maison*.

He was gonna hate me, but I typed a text, held my breath, and hit *send*: *U up?*

It took at least a full minute before the response came. I could practically hear the irritation: *It would appear that I am now.*

I typed in the reply: *Meet me in the employee lounge for coffee at seven thirty?*

He answered: *If you like. But you couldn't have let me indulge in another hour's sleep?*

I texted back: *Sorry. It's just that I'm gonna be busy later today, and I wanted to make sure you could meet.*

No reply came right away, so I took five minutes to rinse off in the luxurious dual-headed massaging shower. I'd really wanted to stand around for twenty or thirty minutes and let the water beat down on me—the thing was more like a spa treatment than anything else. Harry had spared no expense in outfitting the suites when The Mansion had been remodeled into the eclectic-yet-deluxe-themed retreat for eccentric travelers.

The bath products from the Hidden Passage spa downstairs were beautifully laid out on the bathroom counter in white bowls with a colony of bats taking flight. They were the signature soaps, shampoos, and lotions used by the spa and were imported from a hot mineral springs spa in Baden-Baden, Germany. I loved using them and hadn't had all that many chances to do so up until the last couple of weeks when I'd been staying with Jack. His bathroom held those same rich and creamy items that smelled like honey and almonds, and when I stepped out of the shower that morning and wrapped the fluffy resort robe around me, the amazing scents had saturated the steamed air. And Jack was all I could think about.

It was still only a little after six a.m., so I crawled back under the covers, opened my laptop, and Googled Roger Goodwin.

Goodwin's Hollywood heyday had peaked decades ago, after which he seemed to have slid down the power ladder rung by rung until he was flat on level ground with the majority of folks in La-La Land.

The photo on his Facebook page was of a twentysomething, virile, intense man whose dark and penetrating stare was kind of sexy. His IMDb page, however, displayed a Roger Goodwin thirty-some years later who was softer and more tired looking. Goodwin was credited with over thirty films, most of them made in the 80s and 90s. After that, he had one box office flop after another until his list of credits finally stopped about eight years ago.

I found a years-old interview in *People Magazine* just before his Waterloo movie, *Pharaoh's Ghost*, was released. When the interviewer had asked him to sum up his contribution to the film industry, Goodwin had answered, "Contribution? Try: *staggering*. Almost single-handedly, I've rejuvenated box office ticket sales. Hell, I guess you could call me the Second Coming."

The guy doesn't think much of himself, does he?

I had a quick flash of Grandmama Ida shredding the magazine, burning the pieces, and then hurrying on down to light a candle for the blasphemer.

Goodwin's Wikipedia page portrayed him these days as a has-been, and given that, I had to wonder what had made the Powells choose him to make the documentary that seemed so vital to the enhancement of their public personae.

While Roger was in my chair, I intended to quiz him about the Powells. And everyone knew the best way to get an egomaniac to talk about someone else was to first get him to talk about himself. My mama had taught me that. Mama managed

Ruby's Famous Bourbon Chicken, a long-time staple of the Holy Cross neighborhood where I'd grown up. While the chicken was to die for and was the main reason folks flocked to Ruby's from all around NOLA, the other reason was that over the years Mama had always made sure everyone who walked through the door felt like they were going for a dinner of bourbon chicken and fixin's at a friend's place.

She knew all the repeat customers' names and histories, and even if she wasn't working when someone went to Ruby's they always asked after Della. That was why Mama had always done pretty well financially for the manager of a tiny little chicken place in the Ninth Ward—she knew how to engage people, and Ruby knew the value of that kind of employee.

"If you can get folks talking about themselves, you can get 'em talking just 'bout everything else. 'Me, me, me. All about me. You wanna know 'bout them folks? Why sho, I'm gonna fill you in on them, and then I'll tell you some more 'bout me.' It works every lovin' time, my daughter."

It was only one of the hundreds of things I'd learned from Della Hamilton about human nature, and it was one I intended to use on Mr. Hollywood.

When I walked into the employee lounge at seven thirty after having used the employee's locker room to change into my costume, Fabrizio was already waiting at one of the utility tables, his head resting on his hand, a steaming cup in front of him. He'd also already dressed in his work costume.

I poured myself a cup of coffee, snagged one of Valentine's buttery croissants from the warm and fragrant full plate on the counter, and went to sit beside him.

"Sorry I rousted you out so early," I said.

He raised sleepy eyes and blinked. "It was a bit earlier than what I'm used to."

"Thank you for agreeing to come, my sleepy friend," I said. "I wanted to bring you up to date on what I've learned about the Villars."

Fabrizio leaned forward, his pale eyes keen, and I churned out everything I'd picked off the internet the night before.

He was thoughtful. "Is it your considered opinion Percy and Nancy Villars are what they represent themselves to be?"

I lifted one shoulder. "I can only tell you what I learned, but so far I don't have any reason to think they have an agenda other than to find the letter, validate Belle Villars' journal, and write their book."

"I see. Thank you for this," he said.

"Your turn. Did you manage to get over to the gift shop and check into that receipt you came across yesterday?"

"Yes," he said. "I did garner something of the receipt. At first I was discouraged when I learned that the young woman behind the register hadn't been working at the day and time indicated on the receipt. However, she did look up the stock number of the item sold."

"And?"

"I don't know quite how…" His voice trailed off, and his face went from his usual British pallor to a rosy pink.

"What?" I couldn't help smiling. His discomfort was charming.

"The item purchased was uh, er, lady things."

"Lady…? In plain English, please."

He cleared his throat. "I believe the young woman referred to the item as"—he took a deep breath—"tampons," and then buried his face in his hands, showing me the top of his cream-colored turban. I was dying to mention the fact that this particular gift shop check was obviously neither his nor Harry's, but I held my tongue to avoid embarrassing my sensitive, old-fashioned friend any further.

He finally lifted his head and said, "It's a cash receipt as you and I had already determined, and since the clerk wasn't present when the purchase was made, she was unable to enlighten me as to the identity of the purchaser."

"Well, that's a real shame. I'd been hoping we'd learn something, maybe get ourselves a lead or two out of—"

He interrupted me. "We did, my dear. I can't be positive it will turn out to be what you call 'a lead,' but then again…"

"Tell me."

"While the young lady was of no help, the young man stocking shelves overheard my questions and indicated it was he working at that hour, and he remembered the woman. In fact, he said he'd never forget her."

I waited as he played the moment, stretching it for its full dramatic reveal. I'd once heard Fabrizio say, "Old actors never die. They just go into syndication. Once a thespian, always a thespian." Words to live by, I guess.

He continued. "Evidently the guest in question was a stunning woman with bountiful physical attributes that were displayed to their"—he cleared his throat—"fullest advantage in her quite high-riding shorts and revealing tank top."

I looked at him as I digested what he'd said and what it meant. He smiled back at me, his brow creased above his lifted eyebrows, his gaze knowing, and he slowly began to nod his head, encouraging me to make the connection.

"So a curvy woman in short shorts and a tank top bought a"—I cleared my own throat then and spoke quickly over the item that had caused Fabrizio so much consternation—"box of tampons at the gift store." His consternation faded, and his smile broadened as I said slowly, "And *that* was the receipt we found inside *la petite maison*."

Fabrizio sat back and folded his arms over his chest, waiting for me to ask the obvious question.

So I did. "Fabrizio, what the heck was Theresa Powell doing inside the house where Elroy Villars was murdered?"

"Well, now," he said, "that is a bit of a head-scratcher, isn't it?"

"Yes. It is." I checked the time. "Oops, have to go. Mr. Hollywood's stopping by the studio for a tattoo this morning." I stood and leaned down to hug him when I remembered. "How did the séance go last night?"

His chin lifted. "Swimmingly, my dear. Although Belle Villars did not make an appearance, it would appear that Jean Lafitte himself came around to chat."

I grinned at him. "No. You didn't!"

"Oh, indeed." He winked. "And it seemed the scoundrel was quite flattered over all the to-do—indicated if he'd known that one piece of parchment belonging to him could have caused this much a stir, he'd have stashed items hither and yon for the enjoyment and edification of all his admirers."

"Wish I'd been there to see it."

"As do I, dear Melanie. As do I. It was an Oscar-worthy performance. Or at the very least, a BAFTA."

CHAPTER TWENTY-TWO

Mr. Hollywood was right on time at eight thirty a.m., strutting into Dragons and Deities like he had "Stayin' Alive" playing on his Bluetooth earbuds—and when he switched them off and I could hear the music, it was, in fact, the Brothers Gibb warbling their biggest hit ever.

Goodwin was decked out in yet another *Miami Vice* pastel getup, this time baby blue slacks and a pink jacket.

"Mel!" he said, seeming surprised to see me. "It's you! You're the tattoo lady?" He stuck out his hand. "I'm Roger, remember? From the other night when you went inchworming under that house?" He laughed.

"I remember f'sure. It's good to see you again." I tried to be perky, but my level of enthusiasm wasn't anywhere close to his. "You've decided you want body art?"

He grinned. "Oh yeah, baby. And I know exactly what it is I want." He pulled a paper from his shirt pocket, unfolded and handed it to me.

I stood looking at it, certain there was a frown on my face. "What is it?" I asked.

He seemed surprised. "Well, it's a—" He stopped and glanced down at the paper. "Oh, right. No wonder." He took it out of my hand and turned it. "You were looking at it upside down."

I still didn't know what it was. For want of a better description, it looked like a child's cartoon version of a Martian—large domed head with big eyes and multiple arms and legs. "Oh," I said. "You're sure this is what you want?"

He slipped off his jacket. "Absolutely. It's my next project"—then his shirt came off—"and it's going to be massive." He all but threw himself into my chair and pointed to a patch of pale skin on his upper right torso where he'd already shaved. "Right there. I have the exclusive rights to this project, and the tattoo will help me keep focused on it."

"All right, Mr. Goodwin." I got what I needed to transfer the design onto his skin. "You probably want some background flourishes and such, dontcha?"

He nodded. "Yeah, give me the works." He leaned back. "Oh, almost forgot. It's green. Like granny apple green."

"Green," I repeated. "No problem."

I prepped the skin, transferred the design, prepped the skin a second time, switched on the pump, and started.

"Mr. Goodwin, please try to hold still. It'll turn out ever so much better, trust me."

I'd already had to ask the squirming man several times.

Personally I only had one small Tinkerbell tattoo that wasn't very elaborate. When the work had been done, I hadn't considered acquiring it all that uncomfortable. But I was never judgmental of my clients' reactions to the invasive process of having a permanent painting applied to their skin. Some folks handled it without so much as a wince or a flinch, carrying on pleasant conversation while I worked. Others had a heckuva hard time with it, even having to stop and rest in between. Mr. Hollywood's reaction leaned more toward the latter. I was barely into the process, and he was already having trouble, sweating and groaning.

I asked him if he needed to stop and recoup for a few minutes. He raised his eyes to me and replied through gritted teeth. "No. I must keep going. It's for my art." And with that, he turned his head away from me and seemed to be focusing on the painting of a Bela Lugosi-type vampire wearing a tank top that showed he had tattoos covering every inch of exposed flesh. I'd painted it for the salon myself early on in my employment there.

Even as weird as Roger's drawing was, the design was straightforward and pretty basic. It wouldn't take me all that long to get it done. I didn't waste any time broaching the subject I was most interested in talking to Mr. Hollywood about—the Powells.

"So, Mr. Goodwin," I began. "How did you hook up with the Powells? Why did they decide to use your services for their documentary?"

He huffed. "Why *wouldn't* they want to use me? Woman, I'm famous. I'm Roger Goodwin."

Oh, right. I'd forgotten Mama's golden rule about narcissists. "What I meant to ask was why someone as famous and accomplished as you are would decide to work on the Powells' documentary? I mean after *Milky Way Mission* and *Pharaoh's Ghost*? I'm surprised you'd agree to take it."

"I see." His voice sounded more satisfied with the revised question. "Well, this tattoo you're working on?"

I wiped excess ink from the outline of the alien and bent for a closer inspection of the funny-looking little creature. "The tattoo, yes."

"As I told you, it's representative of my new project, my dream project, if you will. The script miraculously came to me, as they used to say in the business, over the transom. Unsolicited. It's a very exciting project. I've been working sort of behind the scenes for a few years now"—*Behind the scenes? From what I'd read, he'd been clean off the map*—"and I accepted the work from the Powells with the hopes that it would remind the industry moneymen that Roger Goodwin is still around, still has what it takes, and is still bankable."

"Oh," I said.

He went on, Della Hamilton's let's-talk-about-me method working perfectly. "The Powells seem to have access to different avenues of distribution. Archie Powell even mentioned that HBO might be looking at airing the film. If not them, they've also had some interest from the History channel. And once everyone sees that Roger Goodwin is back, creative juices flowing like wine, nobody's gonna tell me no when I take them this one." He dipped his chin down to indicate the tattoo taking shape on his chest.

"Well, I hope it works out for you," I said. "And for the Powells too. Taking possession of the Jean Lafitte letter seems pretty important to them."

"Yes," he said. "It does seem pretty important to them. But their success doesn't make one iota of difference to me or to the success of the documentary. In fact, I have an endgame in mind that will work better if they *don't* get their paws on the thing."

"How's that?"

He smiled—wily, secretive. "Plot twist." He lifted his free arm and wagged a finger at me. "Spoilers." He paused only long enough to take a breath before, "Someone told me this place is loaded with hidden passages and that you're the go-to gal to talk to about them—that you got chased around behind the walls a while back. That true?"

Was it ever. I'd never forget the terrifying experience fleeing for my life in the pitch-black maze. That had been a little more than a year ago, but the memory was still fresh, and just the thought still made me shiver. "I did get stuck behind the walls once. Yes. Why do you ask?"

"If I could work it out, you know, get permission from the resort manager, I thought it'd be an awesome location to shoot some scenes. Like maybe the Powells could, uh, be looking for the letter of pardon back in there. Doesn't it sound logical that if the letter was moved from where it was supposed to be, it might have been hidden somewhere else? Like maybe in a secret passage?"

I shrugged. "I guess." But I thought that was really reaching. In my mind, if the letter wasn't where it had originally been hidden, someone had just already gotten to it. And why would that someone bother to hide it again?

I worked quietly for a few minutes, beginning to fill in the Martian dude with varying shades of yellow and green.

Not talking about himself for a couple of minutes must have been getting to Goodwin. "You know, one of these days, sometime down the road, I'd like to make a true-crime documentary about the mystery of the Powells."

Mystery? "What mystery?" I lifted my ink gun to avoid ruining the design if what he had to say broke the case wide open and caused me to do something wild and crazy. "The Powells are a mystery?"

"Mmm." He was having an easier time talking now that I'd momentarily quit inking. "As I recall, it happened two or three years ago. It was in all the papers. Archie and Theresa had acquired an 1860 repeating rifle which was documented to have belonged to Crazy Horse." He lowered his voice and spoke more slowly like he was talking to a six-year-old. "Crazy Horse was the Indian chief who massacred Custer and his men at Little Big Horn."

I knew who Crazy Horse was. Anyone who'd ever gone to school in the United States and had to pass social studies in junior high knew who Crazy Horse was, but I bit my tongue and said, "Thanks for explaining."

"This rifle had been missing for decades but suddenly resurfaced. The man who owned it didn't want to sell it. Low and behold, he up and died mysteriously. The widow needed money and sold the rifle to the Powells for what most people thought was a song. Wouldn't that make a good film?"

A mysterious death and the Powells benefited from it? *Actually, Mr. Hollywood*—"Yes. It definitely would."

CHAPTER TWENTY-THREE

———

Roger—why wasn't I surprised?—"forgot" to leave a gratuity for the work I'd done. But the tip he'd given me about the Powells and the mystery of the dead rifle owner was generous in its own way, providing a new avenue to travel along in relation to the Powells.

I only had one more appointment for the day, and it was a good thing too. It opened the day up so I could do a little more sneaking around and digging into people's lives. Did it make me less of a busybody because Harry asked me to do it? The scant work schedule was Harry being true to his word about blocking me out and giving me a light work load while I was helping him clear his pseudo-relatives Percy Villars and, by proxy, his sister, Nancy.

First I headed for the employee locker room and changed out of my costume back into my jeans and T-shirt. Then I went upstairs to my, ah yes, dee-luxe suite, and ordered an early lunch from room service. While I was in the back wing, I'd gotten a whiff of Valentine's special soup, and by the time I made it to my room, I could hardly wait to have some.

My lunch of Cajun-style Chicken and Rice Soup arrived not more than fifteen minutes after I ordered it, along with some warm, crusty French bread, honey butter, and a tall, frosty glass of sweet tea.

I opened the French doors to the Juliet balcony and sat down to enjoy the soup, always full of big chunks of chicken, scoops of wild rice, and all the right veggies floating in a spicy tomato broth. Delicious.

While I was at it, I set my laptop to the side and Googled *1860 Crazy Horse rifle*, which came up with only sketchy details, little more than Roger Goodwin had given me. It had all taken place in a small town in Montana not far from where the infamous battle had taken place. Further searching through a white pages website and the subsequent nine-dollar ninety-nine-cents fee gave me the name and contact information of the widow who'd sold the rifle to the Powells.

I picked up my cell phone and dialed the number. It went to voice mail. "Hey there, cowhands. You've reached Mabel Ann Gunderson at the Rocking Bar G Guest Ranch. I'm probably out in the south forty right now"—*right* sounded more like *rat*—"or out on the trail at a campfire cookout. Just leave a message, and I'll get on back to you soon as I can." *Beep.*

I left my name and number without mentioning what I wanted to talk to her about.

The soup was all gone, and in lieu of licking the bowl, I used the remaining bread to sop up every last drop.

While I had the laptop running, I went back to Facebook, first to Percy Villars' page, then Elroy's, and finally to the page I'd found for Percy's fiancée, Juliette. I sat several minutes looking at the photos on all their pages. Something just wasn't quite right, and for the life of me, I couldn't put my finger on what it was.

On Percy's page, he and the young woman standing together as stiff and unsmiling as the *American Gothic* couple. Elroy, on his page, laughing and goofing around with his friends. Percy and his fiancée again on her page locked in that hot kiss—

The iconic light bulb lit up over my head. *Light bulb, hmph. More like a spotlight.*

I picked up the resort phone from the nightstand, rang the front desk, and asked to be connected to Percy Villars.

No answer.

Didn't matter. I'd find him. I drained the rest of my sweet tea and headed out to look for him. I needed to talk to Percy, and it felt like I needed to talk to him now.

* * *

Percy was at the patio bar. I had a word for the way he looked, a really good word, one I'd heard Fabrizio use. My friend had told me that when he first arrived in the States before he found his way to Mystic Isle, he'd been lost and lonely and *dolorous*. I'd stopped him and asked what it meant—technically: woeful, miserable. But that Monday afternoon if you'd looked up the word in the dictionary, you'd be likely to find a picture of Percy Villars. Even his big ol' ears were drooping. His eyes were red rimmed and swollen. From the empty collection of hurricane glasses on the table it looked like Percy had opted for a liquid lunch. I got it—his brother dead, his woman gone, his book deal fading away.

Heck, the man was a living, breathing country song.

"Hello, Percy."

He looked up at me—mouth downturned, curly hair standing up in strange little reddish clumps. Even the skin on his face seemed sallow and saggy—like I said: *dolorous*.

"I'd ask how you're doin'," I said, "but it's pretty obvious. Do you mind if I sit with you?"

He looked back down into the tall glass that only held a sip or two more. He didn't say yes, but he didn't say no. In fact he didn't say anything, so I pulled out a chair and sat.

"I wanted to ask you a couple of questions, Percy. About your engagement. I understand you recently broke it off."

Still he just sat there, hands on either side of the mostly empty cocktail glass, head down.

Hmm. Maybe a new tact? "I've seen photos of your girlfriend on social media. She's cute, Percy. I bet you miss her."

Not even a twitch. Was he still breathing? I resisted the urge to reach across and pinch his arm.

"I was a little confused about one of the photos, though." I fished in my pocket for my phone on which I'd left the Facebook app open to the picture I had in mind, the kissing photo that had been tagged as Percy and his girl at the restaurant. "This looks like you with her, Percy, but I don't know. I just have to wonder if it isn't Elroy."

Nothing happened for a beat—two—three. Then it was as if someone had yelled, "Fire!"

Percy jumped up, nearly knocking over the table in the process, and ran away. He was yelling and screaming like a hysterical three-year-old and waving his arms above his head.

Everyone on the patio jerked around in surprise to watch the show.

I bolted to my feet and ran after him, wondering if this was what Nancy had meant when she told Cat she avoided the subject of his broken engagement because he reacted *strangely*.

"Percy." I shouted after him. "You don't have to run away. I just want to talk to you."

If anything, he ran faster.

I was getting pretty winded, and Percy had begun to pull away. That "no exercise" policy I'd been following since completing my credit requirements in high school gym class wasn't working out all that well for me.

"Please," I puffed. "Just stop."

I couldn't believe it, but he kept running—really fast. He sort of had that thing going on that reminded me of the way Tom Cruise runs in all his movies, legs pumping like pistons, arms in perfect rhythm with legs, shoulders down, back straight. I'd never catch up to him—*Mission: Impossible*—except I got a break.

He was heading for Harry's Garden, and I remembered that a good-sized area of that had been cordoned off for the construction.

Thankful as all get out, I slowed down as Percy came to a dead stop at the far end of Harry's Garden and stood looking around as if he didn't know where he was or which direction to go from there.

"Percy." It came out in a wheeze.

He whipped around. "What happened between Juliette, Elroy, and me is no one's damned business." Crap, he wasn't even breathing hard, and he was turning to take off again.

"You're right." I blurted out, stopping several yards away from him. "You couldn't be more right."

He paused and turned back.

"You must have been so hurt when your brother and Juliette turned to each other."

"Turned to?" He laughed. Well, not so much a laugh as a harsh bark. "You think Juliette was in on it? She didn't even guess, except she was ever so hopeful that maybe soon I might

be feeling frisky again like I was with her that one night. Frisky."
He did that bark/laugh thing again.

Elroy had pretended to be Percy and hadn't even told
Percy's fiancée? Oh man, that was really low. The jerk might
have deserved what he got after all, even though I was pretty
sure the law wouldn't see it that way.

I took a mental guess that this wasn't the first time
someone had died when a woman came between brothers. I
didn't really want to ask but felt the question needed to be raised.
"Did you do it, Percy? Did you kill your brother to get even for
the awful thing he did to you?"

Percy opened his mouth to answer, but nothing came
out. He'd focused on something behind me, his face distorted, his
mouth gaping in a silent scream before he was set in motion
again, whirling and scrambling.

I heard it before I saw it—a growl, low and guttural, like
a lion or tiger beginning to think about an out-and-out roar. I
spun to the sound.

It was the pesky gator that'd been cruising the resort,
disrupting, wreaking havoc. Only it didn't look so pesky just then
from where I stood—it looked positively menacing and
completely deadly.

I vaulted out of its way. Even if I was slower than Percy,
I was faster than the gator. It had raised up onto its short but
powerful legs and came scuttling across the lawn, its enormous
jaws partially open, so the dang thing looked like it was smiling
at me. And why not? It had cut me off from getting around it.

"Help!" I managed one yell.

Terrified to take my eyes off it, I glanced away for a
brief look around. There. Off to my side. Salvation—the staging
area of construction materials—pavers, boulders, bricks, other
supplies, stacked on pallets, some covered in thick plastic
sheeting, others uncovered. I launched myself at it, using my
hands and legs to scramble up onto a pile of big boulders then
climb farther up onto the flat tops of the stacked pavers and
bricks.

Just to be on the safe side, I yelled again. "Somebody
help me!"

In the near distance, a delivery van had pulled up outside the resort, and two men were unloading what looked like cases of liquor through a service door that had been propped open with a steel rod. I stood as tall as I could and waved both arms, shouting again. Neither one of the men looked up.

I was scared, but at least I felt like maybe I was out of reach of the humongous reptile, if only for the time being.

My moment of triumph was way too freakin' brief. Not only did that gator not stop, but after a brief pause of what looked first like assessment then like brazen confidence, the crazy thing started up the slope of the rock pile toward my perching spot only a few feet above it.

I had nowhere else to go. "Oh please, help." This time it was barely a whisper.

But it was the one that seemed to work.

A chorus of shouts rang out, male voices, and I took my eyes off the gator to look across the garden lawn.

It was the Gator Brigade, Odeo, Lurch, Ralph from the shuttle bus, and a couple of others—God bless them—God bless 'em all. They were running full-on after the gator, and they were loaded for bear. Or maybe it was alligator they were loaded for.

Whatever. To me they looked like angels from on high. And I couldn't help squealing like a delighted child when their yelling and general overall pandemonium finally caught the attention of the big old thing. It stopped climbing and set up with a series of growls and chuffs, obvious dares. But it did back down the boulder pile and take off in the other direction.

"Hallelujah."

As soon as the way was clear, I began a careful climb down off the pallets of bricks. I hadn't been nearly so careful on the way up, and my palms and knees were a little scuffed.

While the others ran on after the gator, Odeo stopped, threw down his heavy-duty six-foot snake tongs, and reached out two strong arms to help me.

"Oh, goodness sakes alive, Miss Melanie. I was nearly scart to death when I saw you there with dat ol' gator on its way up to you."

I relaxed and let Odeo lift me the rest of the way down as if I were no bigger than an eight-year-old child.

When my feet found the carpet of exquisitely cared for lawn once again, I wasn't surprised to discover I was shaking.

"You okay?" Odeo must have thought I was going to fall down because he reached his big hands in my direction.

"I'm just shook up, Odeo. I'm just all kinds of shook up."

Lurch and the rest of the reptile hunters were heading back in our direction, their heads down, their pace slow.

It looked like the gator had once again made a clean getaway, and Percy Villars wasn't anywhere to be seen either.

CHAPTER TWENTY-FOUR

———

I made it back to the main building on wobbly legs, Lurch on one side of me and Odeo on the other. I thanked them effusively for about the tenth time, and we parted ways.

I went straight up the stairs, hoping to find Harry in his suite. He wasn't there. Neither was Fabrizio.

Back down the stairs. It was important to me that I find Harry and tell him there was a strong possibility good old Percy might have offed his brother after all.

Downstairs, Lucy was on duty at the front desk. One guest was turning to walk away as I approached. *One guest*, not the more than thirty she'd had to wrangle the day before. But then that had been Sunday, a weekend day, when many weren't working and people were free to boogie on over to the bayou and hunt for a missing historical document. Not nearly so many people seemed to be hanging around on Monday afternoon.

She turned and smiled when she saw me. "Hi, Mel." She gestured toward my jeans and long-sleeved Henley. "Not working today?"

"Not since this morning," I said.

"How do you like the suite?" she asked.

I smiled and nodded, wiggling my eyebrows. "Nice."

"I know, right? They're so dreamy. Both Mr. Villars and Mr. Stockton told me to make sure you were well taken care of, had everything you needed. Do you have everything you need, Mel?" Her smile was big and friendly.

Did I? No. I *needed* to be back with my man where I belonged, and I'd take care of that as soon as I could, but right then I was looking for— "Lucy, have you seen Harry Villars today?"

"Oh, sure," she said, waving a hand in the direction of the entertainment wing of the resort. "That good-looking sheriff's deputy rounded up a bunch of people and herded them into the Seeing is Believing Gallery. Harry was one of them."

I caught my breath. There was something going on with the investigation, something I sensed might be quite revealing. And I wasn't part of it? What was up with that?

I thanked Lucy and hotfooted it over to the auxiliary wing. Then I took the short hallway leading into the entertainment section of the hotel which housed the Chamber of Illusion, the Sleight of Hand Parlor, and the Seeing is Believing Gallery. The rooms ranged from large (the Chamber of Illusion), to medium (the Sleight of Hand Parlor), down to the smallest and most intimate Seeing is Believing Gallery where only twenty-four guests were seated within scant feet of the magician.

If Quincy had taken people there, it was to question them—plain and simple.

The door to the small room was open, and I stopped just outside where I could see in.

Quincy stood in the front of the room where the magician would normally perform. In the stadium-style seats rising up from the floor were: Sergeant Pam Mackelroy of the Jefferson Parish Sheriff's office, Archie and Theresa Powell, Nancy Villars, Roger Goodwin, Harry Villars, and Fabrizio.

"Now I've checked the footage Mr. Goodwin so graciously provided from the work that was done Thursday night between twenty-one and twenty-three hundred hours—"

Nancy raised her hand.

Quincy bobbed his head in her direction.

"Twenty-one hundred?" Nancy said in a whiny voice.

"Nine p.m. and eleven p.m., Miss Villars," Pam Mackelroy answered quickly. "Chief Deputy Boudreaux is speaking in official department terms." She threw a look of such adoration at Quincy, when I looked back at him I expected to see he'd sprouted wings, a halo, and a golden aura. How would the good sergeant ever manage to handle things when Quincy was officially off the market?

Quincy didn't acknowledge her but went on. "All of you have at one time or another told me you were present at the site where the documentary film crew was working in the old cemetery most of the night from nineteen hundred to twenty-four hundred hours."

Pam said, "Seven to midnight."

Quincy's mouth tightened in irritation, but he didn't address it and turned toward Harry and Fabrizio. "That excludes the two of you, of course, who were still out of town."

Harry spoke then. "If you realize we weren't even in the state when the murder took place, Deputy, then why have you included us on your guest list on this beautiful afternoon? We have an event taking place here tonight, and my attention may be required elsewhere in the resort to set the stage, so to speak."

"Just outta courtesy, Mr. Villars, just dat good ol' Loosiane courtesy. Dis killin' of Elroy Villars, it took place at your abode, and I figured you'd be wantin' to know all 'bout what happened." Quincy said, slipping back into his thick Cajun accent. I always found it fascinating how he used his ethnicity to his own advantage. There when he wanted to be charming and one of the good ol' boys, absent when he was all business.

"Now—" Without a pause or even a look in my direction, Quincy strolled over to the open doorway, wagged an index finger in my direction, and closed the door, essentially in my face. Behind the closed door, his muffled voice continued. "What I need to ask you all about is…"

"Dang it!" It was a hushed, frustrated whisper as I turned and hurried along the hallway to a storage closet on the other side of the big showroom, the Chamber of Illusion. I opened the door and slipped inside, fumbling over my head for the pull string on the old-fashioned naked bulb light.

A person unfamiliar with the building who went inside the tight space would have thought it was merely a place where extra chairs, display tables, odd props, and other sundry items were stored. But ever since the time of that petrifying experience in the back halls and secret passages of The Mansion, I'd used the occasional break I'd had between appointments at my salon or times when I'd been waiting for Jack to address some issue at the resort to wander those same passageways until they were almost as familiar to me as the public areas of the hotel.

It wasn't just a storage room—it was one of the hidden

entryways into a dark and more clandestine area of the resort that had been part of the original plantation building. And when Harry had discovered them in the older part of the house, he'd incorporated them into the new sections to use as convenient ways for staff to get from one area of the resort to another.

I pushed aside a big shelving unit on wheels and opened the door behind it, finding myself in the dark passageway. Ever since the time I'd nearly gotten lost back in there, Harry had switched the lights from timers to motion sensors, so my progress from the storage room back to an area behind Seeing is Believing was sporadically lit, making me feel a little like Michael Jackson in the "Billie Jean" video. Light. Dark. Light. Dark.

I knew exactly where to stop and listen as Quincy's voice carried loud and clear through the vents. Still, I put my ear to the wall.

"…Goodwin was good enough to provide the rough footage of what you all filmed that night, including shots of the crowd, which was considerable by the way. And I don't blame people for showing up there at all. It's probably a fascinatin' thing to watch a movie get made." Quincy's accent had diminished, and I could tell he was getting ready to do some serious police interrogation.

I heard a murmur of agreement from the others.

Quincy went on. "So when the camera caught shots of you all, again except the two of you,"—I imagined he was indicating Harry and Fabrizio—"that pretty much backed up y'all's alibis."

A dim shaft of light a few feet from where I stood caught my eye. *What?* I slid over to it and was surprised to see a small drywall square separate from the main sheeting attached to the wall by hinges on one side. The light I'd seen came from behind it. *No. Really?* Gently latching on to the unhinged side with the tips of my fingers, I pulled it open. My Grandmama Ida would have said, "Saints be praised," but I didn't want to alert anyone to my sneaky eavesdropping presence, so I just grinned and pushed my face up against the eyeholes in the wall behind what I remembered as a big old oil painting of a woman in an elaborate dress from the pre-Civil War period. It had been done in sepia tones. What was most unusual about the poor woman was the way her hair had been styled. Princess Leia and her Cinnabon hair looked pretty darn normal next to the lady in the painting. This poor thing had three separate sections of hair that had been rolled and piled up until she looked like she was sporting a plate of strung sausages on top of her head.

I figured the sepia-toned lady in the painting now had bright green eyes. But Quincy held everyone in thrall, especially Pam Mackelroy (Cat's own version of Sydney Baxter), and I was pretty sure no one would be looking at the sausage-haired woman in the portrait.

"Has anyone heard from Percy Villars?" Quincy paused, waiting for an answer. "Miss Villars?"

"I haven't seen Percy all day. I looked for him but couldn't find him. I did leave a voicemail. I wish he'd call me back." Nancy sounded worried.

"Well, I do too, Miss Villars. I'd like to talk to him." Quincy cleared his throat and went back to interrogation mode. "I noticed both your brothers in the crowd footage from that night."

I pressed closer to the wall and rolled my eyes as far to the right as possible so I could see Nancy Villars. All the while I concentrated on not sneezing from the dust on the musty wall I'd lodged my nose up against.

Quincy went on. "That was early in the evening, around nineteen thirty hours."

Of course Sergeant Mackelroy felt the need to translate. "Seven thirty."

"There are crowd sweeps you and your brother, Percy, were in, and several neither of you could be seen in. The time stamp told me some of the places I couldn't find you were right at what we in law enforcement like to call—a critical time. The time I mentioned before when the ME believes the murder of your brother took place."

Nancy took in a quick, shallow breath. "Well, sure," she said. "I didn't hang around and watch them move lights and people the entire night. I went out there for a while, so did Elroy and Percy. Then we left for a mint julep at the bar. Percy and I left the bar. Elroy stayed, said he was meeting someone in a little while for a drink. He didn't say who. I don't know where Percy headed off to, but I was tired, so I just went on up to my room and went to bed."

"So Elroy stayed behind, did he?" Quincy's voice was thoughtful. "Did anyone see you, Miss Villars?"

"Sleeping?" Her tone was snide.

"Go into your room." There was no inflection in Quincy's tone. Neutral wasn't something he ever was, so I knew she needed to be careful how she answered.

"How the heck should I know?"

Quincy folded his arms over his chest. "Well, maybe you better ask around, Miss Villars. If you weren't in the documentary footage when your brother was murdered, and no one can verify where you were, that means you don't have an alibi. And that means, your name is still on our suspect list."

Quincy cast a sideways look at Pam Mackelroy, who winked at him then furiously scribbled on her notepad. I figured she'd just written down Nancy's name.

CHAPTER TWENTY-FIVE

———

The good and wily Deputy's next target was Theresa Powell.

"Mrs. Powell," Quincy began, "I noticed there was a fairly long gap in the footage where your husband was on camera without you, and it just happened to be around twenty-two"—he looked at Pam Mackelroy—"ten o'clock. Do you have an explanation of where you disappeared to?"

Theresa ran the tip of her tongue slowly around her lips. Then she smiled a tantalizing, secret smile. Quincy stood waiting, seeming unaffected by the woman's sultry beauty. I couldn't help but be proud of him.

"Deputy." Voice like silk. "I was, mmm, indisposed."

My eyes moved back to Quincy—all cop. "Indisposed? Can you define indisposed?"

"It was a personal matter."

"Personal, Mrs. Powell?"

Theresa looked around the room before lifting one long-fingered hand to her throat. "Certainly, Deputy Boudreaux. I'm having my monthly visitor, and I had to excuse myself to our room for a short while."

I couldn't help noticing that Fabrizio, who'd been silent and motionless the entire time, suddenly buried his face in his hands.

"Do you need me to verify her alibi, sir?" It was Pam Mackelroy.

Quincy gave her a look like she'd just stepped off a flying saucer. "What? No. That won't be necessary, Sergeant." He turned back to the Powells. "At this point, we can take your word for it, and thank you for being so…candid, Mrs. Powell."

"No problem, Deputy. Anything you need. Anything at all."

"Mr. Powell, your turn. When you were off camera for a while during the time in question, what were you doing?"

I had trouble seeing Mr. Powell from my angle, so all I could do was listen as Archie cleared his throat before saying, "I'm well known, Officer. I've published articles in various magazines. In high demand on the speaking circuit. People know me."

"Famous? Huh. And what does that have to do with your absence?" Quincy asked, and I couldn't have put it better myself.

"Fans, Officer—"

"It's Chief Deputy, Mr. Powell."

"Fans, Chief Deputy. I stopped several times during the evening to sign autographs and interact with all my fans."

Nancy Villars spoke up. "I did see him talking to people in the crowd a few times."

"Many of those in the crowd were my people—aficionados of archeology. I owe it to my public to be accessible. Don't you agree?"

While I couldn't see Archie Powell, I could see Quincy, who had a doubtful expression on his face. "Sure. Well, I think that's all I need at the moment. Mr. Villars, I want to thank you for vacating the premises and giving us full access for this extended period. It did help us complete our site investigation. Of course, now you can return to it any time you please."

"Thank you," Harry said. "As Fabrizio and I have nothing to add or refute here, are we free to go?"

Quincy nodded. "And the rest of y'all can be on your way too, f'sure." The charming Cajun was back. "Jes don't be thinking 'bout getting too mobile here for a while. Y'know?"

Murmurs of agreement followed his statement.

"Aren't you going to ask me where I was during that time?" It was Mr. Hollywood. "I mean…come on, you asked everyone else."

Quincy had turned and started for the door but stopped and turned back. "Why, Mr. Goodwin. That's what we always like to see, that spirit of cooperation. But I don't need to ask you 'bout what you might've been doing 'round that time. You were filming, weren't you? Documentaries don't' get made without a director, now do they? And while all these other folks have their motives—fame, fortune,"—he lifted a hand in the direction of the Powells, then Nancy Villars—"Those are things you already have. I can't for the life of me figure why you'd benefit from finding that letter. Not just yet anyway. So if you don't mind, I don't have a single question to ask you right now, but that could change at any moment. I'm goin' ask you to—let me see. How do they say it in Hollywood? I'm gonna ask you to stay fluid." Quincy laughed. "Yes, I think I like that. Fluid."

And with that, he offered the room a big old Quincy Boudreaux grin, turned, and left the room. All the others filed out behind him.

I waited in the dark about five more minutes, giving everyone enough time to leave the area before I stepped out of my hidey-hole.

But when I opened the door to the storage room, Quincy was across the hall, leaning against the wall.

He smiled when he saw me. "*Chère*, did you enjoy the session?"

Well, damn. I felt like stomping my foot. "How'd you know, you crazy Cajun?"

He shrugged. "I caught the change in the light when the panel was removed from behind the painting."

Double damn. "And how'd you know it was me?"

"Aw, *chère*, you like a sister to my lady. You think I don't know those green eyes when I see 'em? Now for da last time, I'm tellin' you to stay outta my investigation." He straightened away from the wall, winked at me, and walked away.

Triple damn.

CHAPTER TWENTY-SIX

———

I stood there for a minute watching him walk away before putting my feet into motion. "Q," I hollered after him. "Wait up. There're a few things I want to tell you."

He stopped walking. "Things like what?"

"Not here," I said.

"Let's head over to the House of Cards. I want to check in with Cat 'bout the party tonight."

"What costume did you go with?" I fell in step beside him.

He looked down at his feet for a moment but didn't break stride. "Cat got it for me."

"And?"

"It goes with hers."

"And?"

"She's Tweedledee," he said, and nothing else was needed.

I tried to suppress the laugh but couldn't do it. "You're Tweedledum? Oh my."

"Mm-hmm. I couldn't talk her out of it."

The idea of Quincy all dressed up in red and yellow and a helicopter beanie just struck me funny, but I could tell Quincy didn't like the idea nearly as much as I did. "Well, I'm sure the two of you are gonna be real cute together."

"Yeah." His voice was flat. "Right."

We went straight to the House of Cards in the main auxiliary wing and had to wait about ten minutes while Cat finished up a reading.

When the door opened and her customer walked out, I was shocked to be face-to-face with Jack's mother. "Mrs.

Stockton?" I smiled and tried to sound as pleasant as possible. "What a nice surprise. Jack told me you were coming." It was all I could do not to cringe away when she stepped closer.

"Oh, Melanie, my dear, sweet child. I'm so delighted to see you again." Was she crying? And more importantly, was she actually being nice to me? She threw her arms around me, and all I could do was stare at Cat, who'd appeared in the open doorway behind her. Cat made a thumbs-up and winked as Mrs. Stockton said softly next to my ear, "I'm just devastated at how badly I treated you when you came to visit. I don't know what I must have been thinking. It was deplorable, and I promise I'm going to make it up to you."

"Uh, well...well...I—"

"Well, I have to run along now. I'm going to the masquerade ball this evening, and I haven't yet picked out a costume." She pulled away and dabbed at her nose with a white lacy handkerchief. "I will see you there tonight, won't I, dear?"

I had absolutely no idea what was going on.

She repeated. "Are you going tonight?"

I nodded dumbly. She patted my hand, and I watched her walk away in the direction of the Masquerade Emporium, her hundred and eighty-dollar peach-colored hairstyle flouncing, her Chico's tunic-top swirling, her block-heeled Naturalizer pumps landing solidly on the carpeted hallway with every purposeful stride.

What in the heck is going on?

"Mel?" It was Cat. "You coming in?"

"That was Jack's mother," I said, knowing I sounded stupid but unable to do anything about it. "Did you say something to her? That was a whole different woman than the one I met in Florida."

Cat just shrugged and turned up her cheek for Quincy's kiss. "She came for a reading. I gave her one." It was the old bait and switch. "What are the two of you up to?"

"If you have a few minutes before your next appointment, we need to tell Quincy what all we know about the Villars and the Powells and the murder."

Quincy frowned at Cat. "We? You've been meddling in the case too?"

"Why, darlin'," she cooed. "Just the teeny-tiniest little ol' bit. Nothing to amount to much."

"You know better," he said.

Her dark eyes narrowed, flashing heat at him. "And you know better than to tell me to butt out. It'd serve you right if we didn't fill you in on what we learned about Nancy Villars…"

The ball was in my court. "…and Percy and his fiancée and the Powells and the mysterious death they were connected to in Montana."

I'd always known Quincy Boudreaux, Cat's beloved, was one smart cookie, and he didn't disappoint me then. He sat down in one of the chairs, crossed his ankle over the other knee, steepled his fingers across his flat stomach, and said, "All right, my beauties. Tell me."

So we did—about everything we knew. Even about the pin and the receipt, both of which he demanded I produce at the earliest opportunity.

I finished with, "For the longest time, I truly did believe Percy Villars couldn't have possibly killed his twin. Then I began to wonder if greed might have made him kill him so he didn't have to split the advance. And now there's this other thing with his girlfriend, Juliette. Greed, revenge, envy, maybe even hate. Serious motives. Right?"

"Good 'n' serious," he agreed.

"I heard Nancy Villars say that Elroy was supposed to meet someone in the bar that night."

Quincy cocked an eyebrow at me. "You mean while you were hiding behind the wall?"

I hung my head and tried to look guilty, but I didn't think it worked. "Yeah. Then."

He shook his head. "No idea. Thought maybe I'd check with the bartender later."

"Oh, brilliant." Maybe I'd beat him to the punch.

My cell rang, and I took a look at the screen. It was a long-distance area code, and I wondered if it might not be the dude ranch lady. I excused myself, got up, and went out into the hallway to answer the call.

"Hello?"

"Hi'ya, this is Mabel Ann Gunderson of the Rocking Bar

G Guest Ranch. I appreciate your patience, young lady, but here I am finally returning your call. What can I do you for?"

I told her who I was and asked her about her husband's death. She didn't offer anything for a long minute, and I was beginning to think the connection had been a dead end. But she finally answered.

"I'm gonna tell you here, Missy, but only because selling that dang old rifle to Archie and Theresa saved my hide when I needed money, and I'm beholden to them.

"Ya see, my husband was a no-good cheating and lying son of a gun. One day while I was out tending the ranch, which was what he should've been about, he died from a heart attack in our bedroom with his trousers down around his ankles while he was with a skanky hooker from over in Billings.

"When I came home and saw how things were, I sent the girl away, and you know I just couldn't bring myself to admit to folks how it had been with him. So I moved things around some, you know, to make it look like the old fool had been drinking and fallen down and died." She laughed. No, it wasn't exactly a laugh, more like a honk. "I musta not done all that good o' job because the sheriff, he was suspicious all right. There was even some talk about whether the Powells had been in cahoots with me, so's they could make a deal for Crazy Horse's rifle my husband had refused to sell them. But the old goat died on his own. Nobody had nothing to do with it unless you want to pin it on the idiot who invented that Viagra."

I thanked her and went back into the House of Cards. "Well," I said. "Doesn't look like the Powells are killers, not as far as the rancher in Montana anyway. That poor old guy bought the farm due to modern medicine."

Both Cat and Quincy gave me an odd look but didn't ask any questions.

"Looks like we're back to Percy and Nancy then." Quincy stood. "The two of you lovelies have uncovered a lot of good stuff here, you know it? And I'm gonna hafta follow up on all of it." He took Cat by the hand, pulled her up from her chair, and kissed her hand. "And I'm gonna start dat right now."

"Right now?" The suspicion in Cat's voice was hard to miss. "I don't like the sound of that."

"I didn't think you'd like it much."

"You're not coming to the masquerade ball tonight, are you?" she said. "Well, dammit all, Q."

"I know, sweet thing." He shrugged. "But what can I do? You and Mel, you done such good work, gave me so much motive and information. My boss, he'd have hisself a fit if I didn't follow up with it."

Cat thinned her lips. "Well, go on then. Git."

His big brown eyes were apologetic but amused as he blew kisses with both hands and left.

"Oh, Cat, I'm so sorry," I said.

She took in a deep breath and let it out. "It doesn't really matter. I know that one too well. He wouldn't be any good to me, just be chomping at the bit to get on with his case. But that just leaves me with one question."

I looked at her, and she went on. "I'm gonna need a Tweedledum to my Tweedledee."

I shook my head. "Aw, Cat. Don't go there."

CHAPTER TWENTY-SEVEN

———

The pirate wench outfit was so cute and sexy and as it turned out, a perfect complement for Jack Stockton's Captain Jack Sparrow costume—and, ironically, we hadn't even talked to each other about our costumes. Unfortunately the pirate wench costume hung in the closet of my room at The Mansion when I waddled through the double doors to the ballroom beside my best girlfriend for life, Catalina Gabor.

At least part of her singular Tweedle status was my fault. So she didn't look or feel foolish, I'd reluctantly consented to be her counterpart.

Yes. That's "Miss" Tweedledum, if you please. The only places the costume had to fit me were the legs, arms, and shoulders, and those parts were all stretchy fabric and not a problem. The rest stood away from my body like I'd swallowed a beach ball. I wasn't feeling exactly glamorous, so of course the first person my gaze fell on when we walked in was Jack.

He looked amazing, just like the pirate Cap'n Jack from my dream fantasy.

The bandana wrapped low on his brow made his eyes more prominent, the black eyeliner either he (or more likely someone else, and I prayed it hadn't been Sydney) had applied dramatically around his amber eyes made them burn like hot coals. Intense eyes, yes, but a sweet and open smile.

He stopped in front of me. "I see we're of like minds."

Were we ever. It occurred to me then that I hadn't seen Sydney Baxter all day. Maybe she'd finally gotten the message and given up, hit the trail, tucked her tail between her legs, vamboozled on outta here. Was it too much to hope for?

The four-piece band struck up Nora Jones's "Come

Away With Me," and he said, "May I have this dance?" and held
out a hand palm up, an invitation in itself.

I went with him out to the dance floor. As usual the
ballroom had been decorated to the hilt. Bats and skeletons and
pumpkins and all other creepy crawlies that come to mind for
Halloween were everywhere. And the tables and other
decorations were traditional orange and black. It was amazing.

Jack pulled me as close as my hooped belly would
allow. We moved to the easy rhythm, and I felt like I'd come
home after a long, tiring journey. "Jack, about Sydney. I know
this has been hard on you too, and I'm sor—"

"No." He said it so forcefully the propeller on top of my
helicopter hat began to spin. "You don't have to say it."

My awesome Cap'n Jack Stockton evidently subscribed
to the philosophy that *Love means never having to say you're
sorry.*

But I wanted to, needed to say it anyway. "I'm sorry."

Neither of us spoke. We were barely moving, mostly just
standing in one spot, swaying. Because of my awkward costume,
his hands were on my shoulders and mine on his sides.

The song ended, but we stayed as we were for a few
beats longer until the band rolled into The Beatles' "Yesterday."

"May I cut in?"

We turned to Jack's mother standing beside us. She
looked just like a flapper from the Roaring Twenties. Lavender
pageboy wig with a sparkly headband that matched the
shimmering, multilayered fringed dress, even a foot-long shiny
black cigarette holder with some kind of fake cigarette with a
glowing orange LED bulb at the end. She looked really good for
a woman in her late fifties or early sixties.

"Mom," Jack said, obviously surprised. "I didn't know
you were coming tonight. I would have come to your room and
escorted you."

She waved a hand at him and laughed. "Oh, don't even
worry about it, son. I wanted to surprise you with my flashy
costume. Are you surprised?" *Who was this woman, and what
had she done with Jack's mother?*

Jack nodded.

"So, what about it?" Mrs. Stockton asked. "May I cut

in?"

"Oh," I said, still standing there with my mouth open like a bass. "Of course."

I stepped back away from Jack so Mrs. Stockton could move in for the dance, but to my complete surprise, and by the look on his face, Jack's as well, she took hold of my hand, put her other one on my waist, and began to lead me away.

I looked around in a bit of a panic. What the *So You Think You Can Dance* was going on? *Oh well, may as well go with it.*

"You look amazing, Mrs. Stockton," I said.

"Oh." She preened. "Thanks. You do too." But her raised eyebrows said otherwise.

"I wore this to help out my friend." I felt the need to explain.

"I understand." It was a simple answer, and once again not the one I had expected from the woman who I'd overheard say to her son, "That girl isn't now and never will be good enough for you."

But I closed my mouth and bit my tongue, liking this woman so much better than the earlier version. I decided not to question it and possibly jinx things.

"Hmm. Oh, look at that," Mrs. Stockton said.

I looked as Mrs. Stockton, leading almost as well as Jack, spun me around so I could see the odd-looking couple across the dance floor.

It was Lurch, a perfect Frankenstein's monster, electrodes and all. Normally over seven feet tall to begin with, the man had added at least another six inches with the monster boots. The person he was dancing with was dressed as—"Oh my goodness, that's a rougarou!" At least from what I could tell, that's what the costume was—an ill-fitting head-to-toe bodysuit partially covered in shaggy brown fur as mangy-looking as Chewbacca the Wookie, four big old paws with fake talons, a head shaped somewhat like a wolf's with a big enough opening between the jaws for the person's face to be fully exposed. The Cajun legend of the rougarou was the equivalent of the boogeyman in other parts of the country. It had been handed down for generations and told many times to warn children they'd better behave. Pretty darn mean if you'd asked me. Why would anyone tell a kid if they didn't do what was expected of them, a big ol' hairy swamp monster would come and get them?

"For the love of Francis Marion," I said, probably louder than I meant to. "Who'd want to dress up like a rougarou?"

CHAPTER TWENTY-EIGHT

––––––

Mrs. Stockton craned her neck for a better view of the bizarrely costumed person who was practically being carried around the dance floor by Lurch. "From what I can see, Sydney Baxter is who. That young woman is just not quite right in the head if you ask me."

This time I couldn't keep it in. "But, Mrs. Stockton—"

"Oh, please, call me Mom."

Mom? Really? "No disrespect, but I thought Sydney Baxter was your idea of perfect daughter-in-law material."

She stopped dancing—I was actually glad, although the woman was pretty light on her feet.

"Perhaps at one time she was, but the tarot cards predict that in the future a blonde with curly hair will send me off to a horrible home for old women that smells like cafeteria food and diapers."

Oh, Cat. I was at a loss for words at Cat's ingenuity, audacity, and fierce loyalty.

"The cards have also foretold how a woman with hair the color of a Gulf sunrise will one day give me beautiful grandchildren and will be kind and loving to me when I'm very, very old and bring me to her home to live. And she will care for me with her own two hands." She sniffed, and I was stunned to see how emotional she was. "That's the woman I need to support."

I thought again, *Oh, Cat.*

Sydney spotted us and headed our way, leaving Lurch standing alone. He waved at her back as she walked away from him.

"Adele!" Sydney exclaimed, reaching out to hug Jack's

mother but finding only empty space as the older woman dodged her.

"What is that you're wearing, Sydney?" Jack's mother asked.

"Can you believe this?" Sydney began. "I had the cutest little pirate wench outfit all picked out, but when I went to the costume store, it had mysteriously disappeared. And they didn't have anything left but this…this…I don't even know what this is!"

"It's the rougarou," I offered lamely.

"The what?" She practically spit it at me. "Well, whatever, I absolutely hate it, but I had to come. I need to spend as much time with Jack as possible."

"No, you don't."

It was Jack, who'd come up behind us. He went on. "What you need to do is leave Mystic Isle. Go home."

Sydney's face, under the rougarou's open jaw with something that looked like fake rubber gore hanging off the fangs, broke into a confused frown. "Oh, Jack, you don't mean that. I've been looking for you all night." Sydney's eyes traveled over him from the top of his dreadlocks wig to the toes of his tall boots. "And all I have to say is *Rowrr*."

Jack flushed, and his eyes went to his mother's face, but Mrs. Stockton only glared at Sydney.

"Sydney, you need to go back to Florida. For everyone's sake, I should have insisted sooner," Jack said. "But I couldn't until now. You need to go home. I'm with Mel, and if I'm lucky, she'll let me continue to be with her for a long, long time."

Emotion nearly choked me. Finally. I wanted to grab his face and kiss it all over. There it was, his declaration in front of the universe—as well as his mother and Sydney—that I was the one, his one and only.

Sydney lifted her rougarou paws and looked at them. Her expression was one of total disbelief. "So you really did mean it? You really do want to be with her instead of me?"

Jack lifted my hand to his lips and kissed it. I could feel the warmth of his lips through the thin fabric of the costume's gloves.

"Do you finally understand?" Jack said.

"Adele?" Sydney looked to Jack's mom for support.

"You heard him." Mrs. Stockton shook her head and lifted her chin, looking down her nose at the poor girl in the weird outfit that was really more like a teed off German Shepherd than a horrible swamp creature who kept bayou children up at night.

"But, Adele, I thought you wanted me to come here to… You said I should… You paid for my ticket. I don't understand."

Adele sighed. "I didn't understand either." She looked at me. "But I do now."

"Well, what am I supposed to do now? Especially since I have this ridiculous JAS tattoo?" Sydney's face looked like a sad emoji with a downturned mouth.

I didn't have an answer for her, and apparently neither did Jack.

But Adele "Mom" Stockton seemed to know exactly what Sydney should do. "Well, Sydney, if I were you I'd be heading to the hardware store back home and asking that nice divorced man who works there, you know, James Sanderson, what his middle name is."

I felt a pang of sympathy for Sydney—more than a pang. Yes, she'd been mean to me. Yes, she'd tried to steal my man. But I couldn't help it. What was happening to her at that moment was sad and humiliating. I couldn't even look her in the eye.

"Well, fiddlesticks." Sydney stamped her paw, tossed her rougarou head, and stalked away, but stopped in the middle of the room and let out a shriek that any rougarou would have been proud of.

"Poor thing," I said.

"Poor thing?" It was Jack and his mother in a duet.

"I can't help it. I feel sorry for her."

Jack dropped a kiss on the back of my neck and goose bumps sambaed around where his lips had been. "Cat's right about you, you know," he said. "You're a real softy—a lovable one."

Lurch, having lost his other partner, clumped over and asked Mrs. Stockton to dance. She twittered, put her small hand in his enormous one, and went off with him just as Nancy Villars, costumed as Little Bo Peep, walked up to us.

"This is quite an event," she said. She eyed Jack. "Don't you look dangerous."

He grinned. "Thank you. I think."

"Have you seen my brother?" she asked.

"Not for a while," I said, debating whether to tell her about his making a run for the border, so to speak, earlier in the day.

"No one's seen him. I couldn't even find him to go with me to the sheriff's inquiry this afternoon. I'm a little worried."

It was totally understandable considering his bizarre behavior.

Jack said, "Isn't that him?"

Percy stood framed in the open double doors. He looked around until he saw us with Nancy and started in our direction. He wasn't wearing a costume, but he did look somehow different. He'd tamed down his unruly hair. Instead of the chinos and golf shirts from the last couple of days, he wore an expensive-looking button-front long-sleeved shirt in a slate grey that looked as if it had been dyed to match his tie and the great-looking slacks that fell in straight lines to the grey Oxfords that carried him across the room. As he drew closer, it began to appear he'd drawn on a moustache.

"Oh, no," Nancy said as he stopped beside her. "Why would you do this?"

Percy lifted his chin somewhat defiantly. "In tribute."

"Well, that's just sick," Nancy said.

"You wouldn't understand," Percy said to his sister.

He looked at me, but before I could ask him why the heck he'd taken off running like Forest Gump, he turned on his heel and walked away.

"Guess he didn't want to come in costume tonight," Jack said.

Nancy sounded disgusted. "Oh, he's in costume all right." She pinched the bridge of her nose between her thumb and forefinger. "He came as Elroy."

"He came as his deceased twin brother?" Jack said. "Well that's just about the craziest thing I've ever heard of."

I had to agree. "It sure is."

CHAPTER TWENTY-NINE

——

Jack took my hand as we crossed back to where Fabrizio was just returning Cat, who was wobbling like a Weeble, to our table after their dance.

Harry and Fabrizio had both donned top hats and tails for the party. They carried walking sticks and wore spats and boutonnieres. Harry was clear across the big room talking to a group of guests. Fabrizio looked like Fred Astaire, and seeing him with yellow and red roly-poly Cat made me smile.

He tipped the top hat to Jack and me. "Good evening."

"You look great," I said.

"Thank you." Another tip of the hat. "How goes the investigation? Harry and I were wondering if further discovery had been made since this afternoon's query by Deputy Boudreaux."

"*Chief* Deputy Boudreaux," Cat interjected softly, but no one except me seemed to be listening.

"Yes," Jack said. "I was sort of wondering that myself."

"Well," I began telling them about my conversation with Roger Goodwin and what he'd said about the Montana rancher dying and how people thought the Powells might have had something to do with it. "But the rancher's wife killed that idea when she fessed up to the fact he'd had a heart attack."

Fabrizio said, "Well, I see what you're saying about their past homicidal history, but that doesn't explain what Theresa Powell was doing at *la petite maison*."

Jack said, "What?"

Fabrizio and I took turns relaying how we'd found the receipt and what we'd learned about it.

When we finished, Jack said, "You're right, Fabrizio.

What the heck was she doing there, especially when you and Harry hadn't been there for over a week?"

As if on cue, Theresa Powell strolled languidly by in her Cleopatra costume.

"Hmm," Cat said. "Walk like an Egyptian much?"

I watched as Theresa passed. Then I turned to Fabrizio. "We could always ask her."

Fabrizio and I walked over to where Theresa stood talking to Roger Goodwin, who looked like a prohibition-era gangster.

"Hello," Roger said. "Lovin' my tattoo."

"That's good," I said then, "Mrs. Powell."

The look on her face was almost comical as she tried to place the butterball standing in front of her, but she must have finally worked it out. "Oh, hello." And to Fabrizio. "Mr. Fabrizio, how dapper."

Fabrizio tipped his hat. He seemed to like doing it. "It's just Fabrizio, and thank you."

Wanting to catch her by surprise, I sort of blurted out, "We're wondering if you can explain what you would have been doing at the house where Elroy Villars was murdered."

My sneaky ploy must have worked because her face went blank, and she began to blink her eyes rapidly. "What?"

I didn't repeat it.

In an even, conversational voice, Fabrizio said, "I don't know if you're aware I reside in that dwelling with Mr. Harry Villars. Due to the abhorrent nature of living there until the proper restorations could take place after that unfortunate incident—"

"Abhor...what?" Theresa asked.

And I offered, "The ick factor."

Fabrizio went on. "—we have not yet returned to the residence except for brief periods. During one such visit, I came across a cash receipt in the kitchen area. It was from the gift shop here in the main building. Queries led us to you, and to ask the question again: What were you doing inside the house?"

By the furrow of concentration between her brows, Theresa had been listening closely. Fabrizio always seemed to have that effect on folks. His verbiage was formally structured and full of high-dollar words, and most people paid close attention. It was one of the reasons he was excellent as the resort's medium—so good in fact, guests who booked séances with him more often than not poo-pooed the disclaimer Harry's legal team had put together regarding the validity of the resort's entertainers.

When Fabrizio finished, Theresa answered right away. "Easy one. Archie and I have let it be known we're here to find the lost letter of Jean Lafitte. When we heard it had been hidden at that location, we went there to hunt around for it. I must have lost the receipt then. But before you even ask, that was *after* the homicide took place, not *before*, and certainly not *during*."

Theresa stopped talking and brushed aside the long black bangs on the Cleopatra wig. Looking back and forth between the two of us, she seemed to be waiting for our response or further questions.

I had no way of knowing what Fabrizio was thinking just then, but it had taken me aback that she'd answered so quickly and seemingly so frankly by admitting she and Archie had snuck over to *la petite maison*.

"Is there anything else?" she asked, looking me right in the eye.

I shook my head mutely and was the one who looked away first. *Yep, girl, you might be sleuthy, but you aren't much on confrontation.*

"Well," she said when we didn't ask anything else, "Archie's waiting. If you'll excuse me?"

I nodded and waggled my fingers in a little bye-bye while Fabrizio doffed the top hat and swept it before him in an elegant bow.

The three of us, Fabrizio, Roger Goodwin, and I, watched her slink away, the silky skirt of her long tunic swirling around her ankles.

"She's quite something, isn't she?" Roger said.

Fabrizio and I both turned and looked at him. Neither of us said anything.

"I'm being summoned," Fabrizio said. My gaze followed his. From across the room, Harry waved at him. "Ta-ta then," he said, this time leaving the topper firmly on his head.

I turned back to Mr. Hollywood, taking a moment to size up the pinstripe suit, white tie, black shirt, and smart black fedora. "Gangster?" I asked.

"Al Capone," he said, first running a finger down the left side of his face where it looked like he'd created a couple of scars by pinching the skin together with Super Glue. "What do you think?"

"Looks like old Scarface to me," I said. "How's the filming coming along?"

"Not bad," he said. "Pretty good in fact."

"Do you still think this one will be your stepping stone to bigger and better things?"

"You bet I do," he said. "One way or another, the missing letter of pardon of Jean Lafitte will facilitate my comeback." He looked out across the room at the dancing couples, the conversation and laughter taking place at the tables. "Yessir, one way or another."

"One way or another what?" I asked.

Roger looked at me. "Well, uh, it's what the documentary is all about now. Isn't it?" He seemed to suddenly remember something. "Say, I haven't heard back from Harry yet. Has he said anything to you about whether he intends to let us film in the secret passages?"

Mr. Hollywood sure was stuck on those not-so-secret corridors.

"You know, Mr. Goodwin, there's nothing all that interesting about the back passages. Just dark hallways. Their original purpose in the old building was for the plantation servants to move around without disrupting the master and his family. The newer ones come in handy for similar purposes. Housekeeping and room service use them. Both the permanent cast, like me, as well as guest entertainers use them for performance purposes. I don't understand why you think that area would make such interesting shooting locations?"

"What if the letter's there? What if I can—*we* can find the letter in there somewhere? That would be, as you said, interesting. Wouldn't it?"

I shrugged. "I would have thought the footage of me coming out from under the house possibly holding this fabulous document that your film is all about would have been key for you, but when I crawled out,"—I shuddered, remembering the spidery, musty, muddy crawl space—"your cameras were turned off. That surprised me."

He shrugged.

"Almost as if you knew the document wouldn't be there to begin with," I said more to myself than to him.

He shrugged again. "Well, as it turned out, it wasn't there after all, so we didn't miss the great reveal. But who knows? It might be hidden in the secret passages. I may still find it."

"You mean the Powells, right? You mean the Powells may find it."

"Either way," he said. "The important thing to me is my comeback. And mark my words. Before you know it, *Attack of the Alien Caterpillar* is going to be the talk at all the conventions. Hell, I'm gonna be bigger than Wes Craven."

Wait a minute. "Did you just say 'alien caterpillar?'"

"*Attack of the Alien Caterpillar.* That's the name of my next horror project. It's all about how things can just really get outta hand if we don't do something fast. The pitch is: *When the organization that's been protecting their species is driven under by corporate greed, a virus mutates the alien worms, and humans are suddenly the prey, not the predators.* Don't you just love it?"

"Was that what I inked this morning? A little green alien caterpillar? Not a Martian?"

"Martian?" He snorted. "No. It was the Lepidoptera Alien Caterpillar." He nodded, pleased with himself, looking about as self-satisfied as I'd ever seen anyone look. "It's going to be huge. The guy who brought it to me is—"

"Incarcerated, by any chance?"

"Why, yes."

"Oh no, Mr. Holly—Goodwin, I don't know how to tell you this, but ironically I've run across this same person before. Many of us here at Mystic Isle have. We had some trouble here at Mystic Isle a while back. Bad trouble, and he was involved. This man isn't exactly what he represents himself to be."

"You know him? Man, what a small world. But don't worry." He waved me off. "I know the whole story already. The guy's an environmentalist who's been persecuted for his efforts to save a species most people don't want saved. He even made me an honorary member of the organization he'd founded to keep the creepy, crazy-looking little maggot going strong—Society for the Preservation of the Lepidoptera Alien Caterpillar. Mouthful, huh?"

He went on, droning about how destructive our species was, how we were destroying the planet, and how the screenplay this guy had written brought all this to the forefront in a scary, funny way that was going to knock everybody's socks right off their feet. "Even better than *Tremors*," he said.

At least that was pretty much what I thought he'd been saying. I was suddenly so distracted I only caught about every third word. What I'd told the director was the truth. I'd definitely encountered the caterpillar guy before, and he really hadn't been what he'd presented himself to be.

But that wasn't what had me standing there unable to focus.

Society for the Preservation of the Lepidoptera Alien Caterpillar. In my mind's eye I was seeing the pin I'd found in the parlor at Harry's place, the letters—SPLAC—designed to curve into letter art. And with that odd little dome at the front, I could see it now for what it was intended to be. The Lepidoptera Alien Caterpillar. I couldn't believe I hadn't put it together before. Granted, the picture Roger had presented for his tattoo only looked somewhat like the real caterpillar.

"Mark my words." He was still talking, oblivious to the fact that I was putting together a scenario where he could be a murderer. "Insects will be here long after we're not around anymore, and I'm going to be the one who brings humanity to that realization, and it's going to make me famous. Famous. And rich as Bill Gates." He grinned. "Well, maybe close." He stopped smiling. "What? Something wrong?"

"No," I managed. Then I took a breath and asked, "Say, Mr. Goodwin, when the Powells went over to Harry Villars' house looking for the letter, did you and your film crew go with them?"

He shook his head. "No. I've never been in that house. I tend not to film beyond police lines. Cops'll confiscate the footage. Doesn't work out all that great."

SPLAC.

I've never been in that house, he'd said. But I knew that was a lie.

CHAPTER THIRTY

Even though I was trying so hard not to, I must have been looking at him strangely. "What's wrong?" he asked.

"Nothing." My voice cracked like a fourteen-year-old boy's. "Nothing. Why?"

"Well, honey, you're looking at me like I just crawled out of that swamp out there."

"It's just…" I couldn't think of anything to say.

The band started up again, this time with "Thriller." At the familiar introductory chords, people who were sitting got up on their feet and began to move toward the center of the room where a dance mob formed. The music was loud and fast, and the guests all cheered and clapped and began to move together in the familiar choreography.

Goodwin was still staring at me.

I took a step back away from him. Two. "Well, it's been real nice talking to you, but I need to…uh…"

"Hang on a minute." He took hold of my arm in a viselike grip. "Come with me. Something I wanted to ask you about those secret passages we talked about this morning." The flat tone of his voice frightened me.

The crowd around us was still moving as he strong-armed me toward a nearby side door. I pulled and twisted, but we were out and moving down the hall before I could react further.

"Too smart for your own good, aren't you?" His voice gritted beside my ear. "How did you know?"

I wouldn't have thought he was so strong, too strong to break his hold on me anyway. "I found your Spee-lac pin. You must have dropped it when you murdered Elroy."

He cursed. "It doesn't matter anymore. You're going to show me these corridors behind the wall and any possible places that letter might have been hidden."

We'd gone a ways back toward the main lobby yet hadn't seen a single soul. Not a bellboy, or clerk, or room service waiter. Where was everyone? It was like we'd left every guest and every employee behind in the ballroom.

I struggled against him. "Why should I show you anything?"

"You will if you know what's good for you or for your friends who live in the house where Elroy Villars died. Those two men are your friends, aren't they? It would be a terrible thing if some night that pretty little house blew up with those two in it."

Oh no. Harry? Fabrizio? Not to mention—me?

My face must have reflected my dread because he shook me again. "Now take me where we can get in behind the walls. That letter was moved from under the house. I don't know when, but I have this feeling I do know where, somewhere in the dark hallways only a very few know of."

I thought he was wrong. He'd never been in the back passageways of the resort. I had and honestly couldn't think of anywhere back there to hide something—unless you took the time to pull down the wallpaper and cut a hole in the drywall. And how stealthy was that?

I led him to one of the back passage entrances.

When we stopped in front of a big wall of bookshelves, Roger said, "Really? Just like in the movies, eh?" He gave me a good shake. "Show me."

I found the handhold and swung out the middle section of shelves to reveal the doorway behind it.

Roger laughed softly and pushed me inside, holding me with one hand and pulling the panel closed behind us. We stood in almost complete darkness.

He cursed again. "Should've brought a flashlight. Can't hardly see anything in here. Why the hell didn't you tell me we'd be wandering around in the dark?"

He shoved me roughly, and I stumbled out into the middle of the hallway-like passage. The motion sensor did its job, and hazy light suddenly spotlighted me.

Roger snorted. "Well, that's more like it. Let's go find us that fortune." He looked back to make sure the access panel was closed securely.

And before he could do anything else, like reach out and grab me again—

I bolted.

I'm not very tall at only five foot three, so my legs aren't all that long, and I'm not exactly an athlete since I couldn't even begin to keep up with Percy Villars. But I had to do something, or people I cared for might die, and anyone who could help me was doing the "Thriller" dance in the ballroom. I dug deep, and the explosion of energy from my short little legs was nothing less than dynamic.

I was halfway down the passage before Roger had even begun to move, but the string of blue language following me warned that I better not slow down—not for anything. I ran. Lordy, did I ever. So fast the spinning propeller on the beanie should have lifted me off the floor—I ignored it. So fast the Tweedledum Hula-Hoop middle banged from side-to-side—I didn't let it slow me down either.

Flashing through one intersection in the hallway, I took the next one to the left. My footfalls were fairly soft, but I could hear Roger's heavier ones coming behind me—that is until I made the next left, which put me back behind the main ballroom. The band's fast and raucous version of "Thriller" was still going on, and the music and crowd noise drowned out any level of racket I could possibly make with just my voice or fist pounding. It drowned out Roger too, but I figured he was yelling at me.

There wouldn't be any help from the ballroom.

And Roger was still coming.

Harry's motion-detector lights were part hindrance, part help. They enabled Roger to see me, but at the same time, I could keep track of him. And at that point, it was easy to see he was catching up.

Even as badly as he wanted to make his ginormous comeback, if Roger decided I wasn't going to help him and was a liability, I didn't think he'd hesitate to hurt me if not kill me.

He hadn't admitted it, but I truly believed it was Roger

Goodwin who'd beaten Elroy Villars so severely he'd died. I wasn't anxious to increase Roger's head count to two.

My heart and the noises from the masquerade ball ringing in my ears, I ran along the dimly lit passage and into the area behind the employees' wing near the main kitchen. That section ended with a door that led outside to the resort grounds.

Hardly slowing down, I hit the door, which opened from the inside but self-locked to the outside.

And then I was on the hotel grounds.

CHAPTER THIRTY-ONE

———

The moon was full and bright in the night sky, and the chilly air cooled my overheated face. I paused only long enough to inhale a deep breath before turning around, grabbing the steel rod they'd used to prop the door open. Only now I used it to jam beneath the handle, hoping to keep Roger inside, at least long enough for me to get to safety.

Something thundered, and I nearly jumped out of my skin.

It sounded like Roger had slammed into the door with all his weight, but the steel rod held—for now. But for how long?

Mr. Hollywood hit the door a second time, and the rod slipped but didn't give way completely. That was enough for me. I took off running again.

I was on the wrong side of the building and too far away from the front entrance to get back there before he managed to come through the door. I headed cross-country. The boathouse was close. I could get there. And if I ran fast enough and slipped inside before Roger broke down my makeshift barrier, he might not even realize that was where I'd run.

The dew from Odeo's immaculately cared for lawn splashed up as I ran, the cold soaking into the tights. The air felt cool in my lungs as I sucked it in. The hairpins holding on the beanie shook loose, and the small cap was flung off my head.

But suddenly I was there, at the boathouse. I pulled open the door just enough to slip inside, and that's when I allowed myself to stop. Finally.

Reaching behind me, twisting, turning, wriggling, hopping, I managed to grasp the pull-tab to the zipper on Tweedledum's rotund torso and yank it down. I pushed that part of the costume to the damp ground and stepped out of it. That left me in the knit body suit with the yellow shirt on top and red tights on the bottom. I stuffed the costume into one of the cabinets near the door.

The bright moon cast pale light through the big bay opening and the few windows at the near end. I'd been in the boathouse a few times before and remembered there was a housephone here. I ran to it and made a connection.

"Bell desk." I didn't recognize the voice, more boy than man.

"Hello? Hello?" My own voice was a hoarse whisper. "Listen. It's Melanie Hamilton. I'm in the boathouse. There's someone chasing me. I'm in trouble. Send help. Send the police."

"Sorry." His reply was slow. "Can you hold on a minute?"

The line went silent. Oh, crap. Nothing else to do but what he asked.

At first all I could hear was the ragged wheezing of my uneven breath as I tried to catch up on oxygen. As my breathing resumed a more normal rhythm, I became aware of other sounds. Boathouse sounds. The slap of water against the wood. The creak of the lifts as the boats under repair swayed beneath them. From out on the water, animals serenaded the bayou with their night songs.

And then there was the sound of Roger Goodwin, pounding across the lawn, huffing and grunting with the effort. How did he know where I'd gone? It didn't matter. He was coming. Coming for me.

I let the phone handset dangle loose, the connection still made, although no one was currently on the other end. Then I whirled to the interior, my eyes flying to every corner. Where could I hide? The last place I looked was up. Just overhead, a medium-sized skiff, maybe sixteen or eighteen feet long, had been hauled out of the water and suspended for repairs. A tarp was slung over part of it, and a rope ladder hung down from it.

I reached and took hold of the ladder, hoisted myself up, and climbed it. Girly-girl that I am with weenie upper body strength, it was a total struggle. I twisted and swayed and jerked and slipped and slid and banged. It was like trying to climb up a bunch of wet noodles.

But I made it, slung one leg over the side of the boat, and rolled inside the small space. As quietly as I could, I pulled the ladder up after me then dragged the tarp across and lay down under it. There was water and leaves and who knew what else in there, but I didn't care. The reason the little boat was in for repairs made itself apparent right away. A shaft of moonlight through a small hole in the bottom of the skiff lit up the inside of my hiding spot. Peeking through it, I could see the door.

If I was quiet and still, maybe I'd get away with it. Maybe he wouldn't find me, and maybe I would somehow see him brought to justice. Breathing a silent prayer, I waited.

The door opened. Roger Goodwin stepped inside. He was holding the beanie from my costume. The traitorous thing had given away my whereabouts. He stood stock still for a moment, and from the angle of his head, I thought he might be listening for a clue as to where I was.

Mouth open, shallow breaths, not so much as a twitch otherwise. I willed my body to stone.

"Oh, girly." His voice was singsong. "Girly, girly, girly."

What? I was being stalked by someone who hadn't even bothered to remember my name? In a way that was sort of an insult. *Knock it off. You're losing it.*

"Come out, come out, wherever you are." What did he think this was—a game? "I won't hurt you. You'll be fine. Not like Elroy. I didn't mean to hurt him either."

He began to edge his way around the floor next to the boat bay. I couldn't see him unless I moved, and I wasn't going to do that. But I could sort of keep track of him by the sound of his voice.

"If old Elroy hadn't been drunk and looking for a fight, he'd be walking around today. But no, buy the guy a few drinks, and he got sloppy. But he told me where to look for that blasted letter."

I could hear the sound of Roger ascending the stairs to the storage area. His voice was farther away now, but I didn't move. Not yet.

"Then the fool up and followed me to the Villars house. Nothing worse than a mean drunk. I was trying to find the letter, and he kept trying to hit me."

Now Roger was coming back down the stairs.

"I didn't intend to hit the guy so hard, you see. And I would never do that to a woman. He just wouldn't back off, and that bathroom paper holder, the wrought iron free-standing antique-y thing, was just so handy. So come on out, little cutie. You know, you're good-looking enough I could make you a star. Petite little redheads do well in the movies. You noticed that? Why do you think that is?"

The sound of his steps stopped, and I could see him standing back by the door.

"What a fiasco this turned out to be." He sounded disgusted. "All I wanted was to beat the Powells to the document. Plain and simple. The money from that piece of parchment would have let me finance my feature on my own. Wouldn't have to crawl around on my knees any more begging jackasses for nickels and dimes. I couldn't believe somebody else got to it first. Where the hell is it? Do you know, girly?"

He waited a moment or two before going on.

"Even Elroy thought it was still there. He was carrying around that pathetic page out of his journal, just waiting for Harry to come back to town so he and his brother could go and get it."

Roger was looking around again, his head turning every possible direction but up. *Please, don't look up. Please, don't look up. Please. Don't.*

And then he was just standing there, his chin sort of resting on his chest.

"Hmph." It had the sound of confusion. "Where'd you go?"

And then he put his hand on the door handle and opened it, having one final look around before stepping back out onto the approach to the small dock.

The door closed behind him, and I heard his footfalls carry him off the wooden deck and back, I assumed, onto the grass.

I waited what seemed like a very long time, but was probably only a few minutes, before climbing down out of the skiff while silently thanking it for serving so effectively as my place of refuge.

I was drained. Barely able to stay upright. It was more than exhaustion. It was depletion. But I had more to do. Since no one had responded to my call for help, I had to get back to the main building and put out the alert that Roger Goodwin was a killer, and he was on the loose.

I opened the door and peeked out. *Nothing this way.* Looked the other way. *Ditto here.* I stepped outside

Aw, hell. No.

This time when I looked back toward the main building, Roger stood halfway between me and the hotel, and he was looking right at me. How the hell had I missed him the first time?

CHAPTER THIRTY-TWO

———

I spun, looking for a way out, an escape route.

A ways from the boathouse and pier, on the sloping bank, Bayou Bill had parked the two four-passenger airboats he used to take tourists out on the water.

Bill had just recently begun to leave his airboats at The Mansion. Bill and Harry had worked out a deal where Harry got a spiff from the bayou tours Bill ran out of the resort. Business was booming for Bayou Bill's Airboat Tours, and from what I'd heard over seventy-five percent of his business came from Mystic Isle—I guessed it was easier for him to leave the boats here and just load 'em up right on the bank.

Their agreement was coming in handy for me just then.

I broke into a run in the direction of the airboats, which carried me across the bank and away from Mr. Hollywood.

He broke into a run at the same time. But our paths wouldn't intersect. I was moving too fast and was closer to the boats, and I got there way before he did.

I slowed down to flip the battery switch then circled around and climbed up onto the pilot's seat. The key was under the seat cushion just where old Bill left it.

I turned on the engine, revved it, and pushed the rudder stick. The boat began to glide toward the water then splashed in.

I put my foot down on the throttle, picking up speed. Granddaddy Joe had taught me to run an airboat back when I was nine years old. He'd take me out to Pontchartrain just north of NOLA where his friend Toby ran an airboat tour company. Joe and Toby and I would take one of the airboats out to the swamps and fish.

It didn't figure that a Hollywood director would have the

chops to hijack an airboat and chase me out on the pond.

I revved up to only about ten or so miles per hour, in no big hurry. My plan was to just cruise around out on the pond until help came. I *had* called for help, after all. Eventually someone was bound to come.

Or maybe not.

When I backed off the throttle, the sound of a second high-revving motor made me put my foot back down and veer out into more open water.

It was Roger of course. Why didn't he just give up and go on the lamb like other respectable criminals? What was I going to have to do to get rid of him? Feed him to the gators?

The channel from Mystic Isle Pond that led onto the lake was about a mile and a half long. The park service kept it clear and navigable, but at night only a crazy person would throttle it up all the way. The shallow draft on these boats might have been great in a few inches of water and in some cases even on land, but if you couldn't see where you were going, there were a lot of ways one of these could get stuck.

Taking it easy was the smart thing, even if there was a crazy man coming from behind at double my speed.

How Roger managed to get the airboat started and out in the water, I couldn't even begin to guess. Because the way the thing was zigzagging and fishtailing all over the place, he couldn't even keep the rudder steady. He'd veer one way, over correct, get the thing up on one side, somehow manage to get it back flat on the water again. Then he'd swing it just as far the opposite direction. He was making rooster tails.

It was like something you'd see on TV. But any minute I expected him to do one of two things, run smack into a mangrove tree or flip the boat. Either way, he'd be off my back.

Since Roger had decided to come after me, my plan just to circle around out on the pond had obviously changed. Now my thoughts were to lead him along the channel to the lake where I could ditch him and make my way back to Mystic Isle Pond.

But Roger "Mr. Hollywood" Goodwin hadn't read the script. He opened the airboat up all the way, which meant I had to do the same or get run over.

I pushed my foot down a bit more until the drone of the motor and propeller sounded like a million angry wasps. We must have been doing upwards of thirty or thirty-five miles per hour then. The moon on the water blurred to a streak of ghostly white. The slight chill in the air turned cold against my face. The flume of spray from beneath my vessel kicked up.

I kept looking behind me to see what Goodwin was doing. By the looks of the spray, he was actually going much faster than I was, but he was so out of control, the gap between us hadn't closed.

I cleared the channel. The roar of my engine and propeller beating the air scattered hundreds of birds from the trees into the night sky.

And then I was on the lake, the open water before me. The urge to smash my foot all the way down and get the hell away from that crazy man was strong. But at high speed if I missed seeing a tree branch sticking out of the inky water, it would be a disaster. I did pick up speed, but only a little.

Roger Goodwin went pedal to the metal. His airboat burst out of the channel onto the lake at an alarming speed. He was getting the hang of the rudder stick and had quit zigzagging. I was suddenly worried that if he got too good too fast at steering the boat, I might not be able to lose him.

In the moonlight I could see him coming toward me, closing the distance between us now that he had control over the boat. He must have had it floored. I could even hear its roar over the sound of mine.

If I could get back up the channel even a couple of minutes before Roger, I could ditch the airboat on shore and run for help at The Mansion. Another *if* was that if the bellman who'd answered my call for help had any brains at all, maybe people were out looking for me already.

I swung around in a wide circle to head back up the channel.

Roger didn't like my move. He countered with a wide turn to come straight at me across the water.

Fast.

If he T-boned me, I'd get the worst end of the deal. Even if I opened the boat up all the way, he'd still hit me.

The white spray of water behind him translated to a tsunami in my frightened brain. He was moving so fast I'd begun to bounce a little. A collision at that speed and the boat would splinter around me. I'd be hurt bad, maybe even killed—we both might be.

Fear fluttered inside me on nervous butterfly wings, sending adrenaline through my system, and I reacted instinctively—or maybe not instinctively because I heard Granddaddy's voice. "Say, Mellie gal, you remember how we used to go night fishing?"

I found myself nodding and saying out loud. "Light up the night."

"Oh yeah. Light up the night." Granddaddy sang it in my head.

I reached to flip on the high beam fog lights and fought the urge to go faster. Instead I eased my foot off the throttle, and the boat slowed, sending a blaze of light out over the water directly at the other boat.

I could see Roger like it was daylight. He threw up one arm in front of his face, blinded.

Then, like it was happening in slo-mo, Roger yanked the rudder stick—hard. His boat jerked and careened away from its bullet path, tipping onto one side. It went airborne and sort of hung there for a few beats. Roger was launched over the water, arms outspread, legs kicking just as the boat flipped completely over.

He crashed down into the water thirty or so feet from the disabled boat.

I lifted my foot even more, and the boat quieted enough that I could hear Roger yelling. My light beams found him thrashing around in the water.

"Help. Help me."

Yeah, I thought, *right*.

I circled the boat slowly around him, not sure pulling him out of the drink would be such a good idea.

His head went under, and the sound of his gurgling cries told me he was swallowing lake water, but he came back up.

My intention was to just circle and keep an eye on him until someone else came to help me get him out of the water.

But then I notice a big ol' gator slide from the bank into the lake, then another, then a third. I must have been sending them telepathic messages back when I wished him to be their dinner.

Aw, man, I'm gonna hafta save the despicable scum.

I slowed to a crawl and maneuvered up to him, climbed down from the pilot's perch, grabbed the boathook, snagged Roger's Al Capone jacket, and dragged him over to the boat.

He wasn't much help getting on board, and by the time he lay facedown on the flat front end of the airboat, he seemed barely able to move. I wasn't taking any chances.

Over Roger's weak objections, I hog-tied him with a length of rope from the safety kit. By the time I was done, I'd used just about all my energy but managed to climb up onto the pilot's seat and head up the channel toward the pond. My hand was unsteady on the rudder stick. I was cold and shaking. My teeth rattled.

My head said—*Stop the boat and curl up on the bench seat*. But my gut said—*Finish what you started*. I kept going, but it was hard.

I rounded a bend and for an instant was blinded by the sweep of a searchlight. A sheriff's boat. The bellman had sent help after all. He'd been a little slow on the draw, but I still owed him dinner and a free tattoo if he wanted one.

Quincy's voice sounded mechanical on the speaker. "Stop the boat, *chère*. We'll take it from here."

But when the sheriff's boat pulled up beside me, it wasn't Quincy who stepped onto the airboat and snatched me off the pilot's seat into his strong, reassuring embrace.

"Oh, Jack." I burst into tears.

CHAPTER THIRTY-THREE

———

Jack sat on one side of me, still wearing the pirate garb, and Cat on the other, my twin in the red and yellow leotard undersuit, on the edge of the four-poster bed in my junior suite.

I'd just finished telling Quincy everything I could remember about what had happened from the time Roger Goodwin told me about the alien caterpillar until the moment I literally saw the light as the sheriff's boat came to my rescue.

Now it was Quincy's turn. "Well, old Roger is already singing like a canary down at the jail. He's given a complete confession of how he wanted to find the letter for himself so he could be some kind of Hollywood big shot again. So he made it a point to get up next to the victim, bought him some drinks, and got him to talk about where he thought that Jean Lafitte document was hid."

Still feeling the aftermath of what I'd gone through, I couldn't suppress a shudder. Cat patted my hand.

Quincy finished up. "Roger said Villars told him the letter was at the house but refused to share the actual page. So once he left Elroy that night, Roger went straight to Harry Villars' place and broke in to search it."

"What about Elroy? How did Roger kill Elroy if he'd left him at the bar?" I was confused. Who wouldn't be?

Quincy gave me an impatient look. "Roger didn't know Elroy had followed him until Elroy burst in. He's insisting Elroy was drunk and kept punching him. Roger just got tired of it and hit him with the TP stand. According to Roger, Elroy hit his head on the tub and didn't get up. But the ME's report says way more than that happened to poor old Elroy."

The thought of such vicious fury shook me. "And Roger

almost got me too."

Jack took hold of my hand and kissed it.

Quincy nodded. "Roger took the page off Elroy's body and went under the house to look for the letter. It wasn't there, so he just threw the page to Belle's journal in the bushes and left. And that's it. We'll be draggin' the pond for the antique paper stand. And they tell me Goodwin's wanting to call a Hollywood agent instead of a lawyer. Something about wanting to get a book and movie deal out of this. Man,"—Quincy ran his fingers through hair that was already standing straight up—"what's this ol' world comin' to?"

Jack pulled the blanket up closer around my shoulders. "Does Roger have the letter?"

Quincy shook his head. "Not thinking he does. Roger said he didn't know Elroy was dead, and before the drunk woke up, he wanted to get the letter and get outta here. But when he went under the house—no letter. I don't think he has it."

"No. He was desperate to find it tonight. He doesn't have it." My voice sounded small and tired, even to me.

"Wonder where it is," Cat said. "What a mystery that is."

"Well, I'm gonna leave you to rest, Mel. You had a rough night. But maybe now you're gonna pay attention when I tell you to keep outta police matters."

Cat got up off the bed. "Yeah sure, sweet man. You keep saying that, but then when the case gets solved, you're happy." She waved a hand in the air. "You know it's true."

"Maybe so, maybe not. But I gotta keep sayin' dat." Quincy crooked a finger at Cat. "Come along, darlin'. I'm gonna have one of the boys take you across home. I'll be along directly."

Cat stood and rubbed her hand softly over the top of my head before taking hold of Quincy's hand. They walked out together and shut the door behind them.

Jack stood, leaving me feeling cold and alone. "I'm gonna start the shower. Let's get you warmed up."

He left me alone while I showered, my head against the wall as the steam enveloped me and washed away all the fear and negative emotions the night had brought.

When I came out of the bath, my head wrapped in a

towel, my body in the fluffy hotel robe, Jack was sitting in the armchair, waiting. He'd taken off the dreadlocks wig, and I was having trouble dealing with the eye makeup and short hair combination. But for all I cared at the moment, he could have been made up as Ronald McDonald. I was so glad he was there with me.

"Will you stay?" I asked. "With me?"

"Whatever you want." He stood, and I was once again aware that he felt a little awkward, but that was the last thing I wanted.

I unwrapped the towel from my head, pulled back the bed covers, and slid in between them, still wearing the robe. Locking my gaze with Jack's, I patted the empty spot beside me.

Jack stripped down to his boxers and T-shirt, crawled in, and turned on his side, slipping one strong arm beneath and one over me so I was wrapped up in a Jack Stockton Snuggie. I scooted so close we could have used a twin-size bed.

"I want to explain about Sydney. And Mom."

I reached up and put my finger against his lips. "Please don't. Not yet. Not tonight. I just need you tonight, nothing else."

He reached for the duvet and pulled it up over both of us. We slept in each other's arms all night.

When I opened my eyes Tuesday morning, the sun slanting through the shutters let me know I'd slept in. Jack's eyes were open, and he was looking down at me. Sometime during the night he'd taken off his T-shirt, and his bare chest was part of what was keeping me warm.

"Good morning." Reluctantly I pulled away a little and reached out to stretch.

"Good morning, but not for long." He smiled, his teeth white against the morning growth of his beard.

I glanced at the clock on the nightstand. "Oh, gosh. Is it really ten thirty? I'm keeping you from work."

I threw off the covers and started to sit up, but he pulled me back down.

"You wouldn't let me last night, but this morning I really want to talk to you about Sydney."

"Jack, it's okay."

"No. It's not. You didn't understand, and every time I

tried to talk to you about it—"

"I shut you down. Jack, I'm sorry. I acted like a spoiled brat, and I promise I won't ever do it again. I don't understand why I was so insecure, but I'm not anymore."

I took in a deep breath to say more, but it was his turn to shush me, his finger against my lips.

"I don't have any feelings for Sydney, not anymore. Like the song says, she's just someone I used to know. I wanted to send her packing right away, but because of how things ended in New York, I had to wait until I could talk to Harry about it. Then there was the murder, and Harry had more than he could handle, and I couldn't bring myself to burden him with…"

"I get it," I said, remembering how Jack came to be the general manager at The Mansion at Mystic Isle.

He'd held the same title at some fancy Manhattan hotel but was unceremoniously let go without references when he'd been unfortunate enough to have been seduced by a beautiful blonde. The one night stand turned out to cost him his job when the blonde turned out to be the much younger wife of the hotel chain's CEO.

No wonder he hadn't wanted to risk something similar by mixing his personal problems with business without talking to the owner first. I remember what he'd told me the first time I asked him to send her home: "Mel, she's a paying guest."

"Glad she's gone," I said.

"Me too," he said.

"But what I'm wondering is how she's going to explain your initials on her body to her next boyfriend."

He looked at me in surprise, the eyeliner from the night before making him look a little ghoulish, but a more handsome ghoul I'd never seen. "She had my initials tattooed on her body?"

I shrugged. "Left shoulder."

"Whoa," he said. "I never knew."

"Good info," I said. "Thanks for sharing."

"And about my mom," he said. "I really did talk to her in Florida, but for some reason it didn't stick. That's why I flew her out here, to make sure it took this time. It made me sick that she was so mean to you. But before I could talk to her about it, something had already changed her mind. She seems crazy about you now. Maybe she could finally see with her own eyes how much I love you."

I knew that wasn't the reason, but still, hearing him say those words sent a thrill from my head to my toes and back up, stopping at my heart which swelled with love for him. I said the words back, "And I hope she could see how much I love you, Jack."

He grinned and leaned down to drop a light kiss on my lips, his bare chest against my shoulder where the robe had fallen partially open.

We spent the rest of the morning lingering over Valentine's Andouille and Sweet Potato Frittata—yummy. Then we shared the awesome steam shower and lingered in there— that was pretty yummy too.

CHAPTER THIRTY-FOUR

We went downstairs together. He went one way to his office in the business wing, and I went the other to the auxiliary wing and the House of Cards.

Cat was just wrapping up with a customer, an older man with a light brown beard and a black toupee. His red plaid shirt and green striped pants made me sorry I wasn't wearing my sunglasses. He looked pretty happy when he walked out, and I had to wonder if she'd told him it was in the cards that his color-blindness would soon be a thing of the past.

"Hey, girlfriend," she said when I stopped in her open doorway.

"Hey."

"How're things this morning? Settling down?"

"They are. Jack stayed with me last night."

She laughed and winked. "Well, that doesn't necessarily mean things settled down, if you get my drift."

Cat knew me and my addiction to Jack Stockton's kisses too well.

"Cat, I wanted to ask you about Adele Stockton. From what she said, I have the impression you sort of predicted a future of geriatric bliss and well-being with her future daughter-in-law who ironically sounded a lot like me."

Cat examined her fingernails, which were as perfect as the rest of her, so I knew she was just pretending. "I might have said something to that affect. Would you hate it awfully if I had?"

I needed to think for a minute. Did I hate it? Maybe, but only because Jack's mother had to be tricked into liking me. I would have much preferred it if she'd come to that on her own.

When I didn't answer right away, Cat smiled at me. It was her kind, understanding smile, and I felt oddly more like her student than her equal when I was the recipient of that smile. "You're a very nice person, sweetie. More than nice. You have so many positive traits, I couldn't even begin to list them all. When not-so-nice things need to happen, well, that's where I come in. I don't mind blurring the lines a bit." She held up her index finger and thumb with a hardly discernible space between them. "Yes, I told Adele Stockton you were the best choice for her, which makes you the best choice for Jack. And that's not wrong. You are."

"Thanks. I guess." But I still wasn't sure.

"And is the blonde bimbo out of the way for good as well?"

I narrowed my eyes. "Yes. But that was all Jack. You didn't have anything to do with that." I stopped, remembering Sydney had mentioned the pirate wench costume had her name on it but turned up missing. Was it the same pirate wench costume Cat had snagged for me? "Did you have anything to do with it?"

"Well, in the end, no. And I thought she looked kind of, well, fetching in the rougarou getup. Didn't you?"

And there it was. I could just see the fearsome four—Cat, Lurch, Stella, and Fabrizio marching arm in arm like the foursome from the *Wizard of Oz* traveling down the Yellow Brick Road. "That's what you guys were doing at the Masquerade Emporium that night."

She lifted her hands, palms up, in a what-can-I-say sort of gesture. "I love you, Mel, and I have your back. Even if you don't always know it."

"Quincy's in more trouble than he can even begin to imagine." I walked around her table, and we hugged. "I have to go meet Harry for coffee and thank him for letting me stay in the hotel the last few nights."

"Oh," she squealed. "You're going back to Jack's?"

"I'm going back to Jack's." *Where I belong.*

* * *

I checked out of the junior suite and asked one of the shuttle drivers to come around and take my bag back to Jack's cottage. I couldn't wait to be back there with him.

It was a glorious October morning on Mystic Isle. Cotton candy clouds in the sky, a light breeze, mild temperature—not too cool and not too warm.

Harry was waiting for me on the garden patio where he'd had iced tea and some of Valentine's tiny little egg salad sandwiches brought down for us to share.

He stood and gave me a half-bow when I walked up. Old school, and I loved it. "Hello, Miss Hamilton," he said. "I hope today is a much better day for you than yesterday turned out to be."

I sat down and picked up one of the little sandwiches. Yes, sure, I'd just had breakfast with Jack barely more than an hour ago, but Valentine's egg salad wasn't anything to be sneezed at.

"I hope so too," I said, popping the mini-sandwich into my mouth. "I want to thank you for allowing me to stay in the gorgeous suite the last few nights and to let you know I've checked out."

"So you and Mr. Stockton have smoked the peace pipe, so to speak?"

My face grew warm, and I knew I was blushing. "So to speak."

"Well, I'm glad to hear it."

"What's going on with your relatives?" I asked.

"You mean my pseudo relatives?" He said it with a smile, but I thought there was a bit of a cynical undertone there.

"Are they going to stay around and keep looking for the letter of pardon?"

"The young lady, Nancy, is returning to her home in Chicago. The brother, Percy, he thinks he might just rent out a place in Gretna or somewhere close and keep looking. I've asked him to let things quiet down some before he renews his search. It got just a little bit crazy all around here, what with everyone goin' round trying to find this so-called historical document." He shook his head as if such goings on were just too much commotion for him to handle. "He's agreed."

"Well, that's good."

"Miss Hamilton, I'd like you to know how much I appreciate your efforts toward solving this matter so Fabrizio and I and even Percy and his sister can get on with our lives. And don't think I don't realize the jeopardy we might have been in had you not stepped to help and save The Mansion at Mystic Isle. We'll be moving back home tomorrow after the place has been gone over good and proper by a professional restoration and cleaning company." He paused, looking away at something over my shoulder. "I'm hoping things will just get back to normal after… What is goin' on?"

He stood and squinted against the sun, even lowering the brim of his skimmer to shade his eyes.

I turned around, and low and behold, my old nemesis the marauding gator was on its way in our direction, scrambling about as fast as it could go.

Praying it didn't have me in its scent like the one always chasing Captain Hook, it was all I could do to not climb on top of the table.

But it didn't seem interested in either me or Harry just then. It ran right by. The gator brigade straggled a ways behind, not nearly as enthusiastic as I'd seen them in the past.

"Why does that gator always hang around this spot?"

Since it didn't seem to want anything to do with me, I got up and trailed along behind it—a long way behind it, mind you—and watched as it disappeared beyond one of the fabric panels the construction crew had hung to hide the work going on.

About that time, two park rangers pulled up in a closed-in truck and got out carrying a couple of catch poles.

The gator brigade came up behind them, and now there were six of us standing around watching the park rangers move in on the under-construction water feature.

One used his catch pole to pull the shade aside.

"Anything?" the second ranger asked.

"No."

"What the heck's wrong with this gator, anyway?" The second ranger sounded irritated. "Doesn't she know it's about time to hibernate?"

"Guess not."

The two men looked at each other then and eased on behind the drape. We could see their shadows moving around back there.

"Holy crap!" one of them yelled. "Watch it. There she is."

"Careful." It was the other one.

And suddenly all hell broke loose back there. Cursing. Growling. Hissing. Thrashing. Stomping.

The six of us—the Gator Brigade, Harry, and I all fell back quite a ways from the site.

It only took a few minutes before the drape opened again, and the two men came out from behind the drape.

"Did you boys get it?" Harry asked.

The first ranger took off his cap and wiped his brow. "We did. Shot her up. She's, uh, taking a little nap. We'll get her and her eggs moved outta there in no time at all."

"Eggs?" Six voices rose nearly in unison.

"Mm-hmm. That's why she's been hanging around terrorizing your guests. She has a nest back there. Silly thing didn't seem to know she's out of season. They usually mate in the spring."

The second ranger added. "Once we get her and her coming brood moved, you're gonna want to go back there and clean that place out, see if any of that stuff she padded her nest with needs to be returned."

"Stuff?" We all sounded like a bunch of monosyllabic idiots.

"She's been taking things from here and there and nesting."

Harry and I looked at each other.

"The gator?" Harry said.

I shrugged. "Maybe. What do you think?"

He said, "For one, I'm gonna be pretty darn interested in what we find in that nest. You?"

I nodded.

"And right now, I'm wondering if that gator had anything to do with the holes I had to have filled in around the stem wall of *la petite maison*. Like maybe she'd been crawling around in there, like maybe she'd been looking for things to carry off and make a nest for her babies, like maybe—"

"She's the sneaky little thief who carried off something half the population of the City of New Orleans and just about every other treasure hunter within five hundred miles has been looking for?"

* * *

Late that afternoon, after the gator and thirty-five eggs had been relocated to some safe place deep in Barataria Preserve, Harry held a ceremony in his garden out by the construction site.

That man just had good old-fashioned style. He arranged for a hosted bar of mint juleps and fancy hors d'oeuvres with a jazz trio playing in the background. The event was well attended, including all the principals—Archie and Theresa Powell, Nancy and Percy Villars, and even Roger Goodwin's film crew that the Powells had paid to stay on. Some of the employees, like Cat and Valentine, and even Deputy Quincy Boudreaux—sorry—Chief Deputy Quincy Boudreaux showed up more out of curiosity than anything else.

Adele Stockton, dressed up like Sunday-go-to-meeting as Mama would say, had decided to hang on my every word. Be careful what you wish for.

Precisely at five thirty p.m., after a drum roll, Harry pulled aside the drapery hiding the construction site, and he, Jack, Odeo, and a few other maintenance crew members went inside carrying a big empty basket between them.

We were all far enough away that we couldn't really see where they went to get to the gator's nest.

The jazz trio played, and the crowd milled around enjoying the festive mood.

After about fifteen minutes, the five men came back from the fenced-off work area. The two men still held the big basket between them, but it was no longer empty.

And what lay on top of it made me gasp, Archie and Theresa Powell shriek, Nancy Villars clap her hands over her mouth, and Percy Villars utter, "Oh, Elroy. If you could only see," before he began to cry.

It was a weathered leather folder that looked very much

like what I perceived a document case from the 19th century would look like, and I knew that when it was unlaced, they would discover a cracked and faded letter from President James Monroe to the Governor of Louisiana on behalf of one privateer, mercenary, and scoundrel, Jean Lafitte.

And some chilly night, if a little comfort food is what you're craving, give Valentine's spicy recipe a try with a warm, crusty baguette.

Valentine's Cajun-style Chicken and Rice Soup

Prep: 25 min.
Cook: 2½ hours, plus cooling

You'll need:
1 broiler/fryer chicken (about 3 pounds)
10 cups water
2 teaspoons salt
½ cup uncooked wild rice (may substitute long grain rice).
½ cup chopped onion
½ cup chopped celery
½ cup thinly sliced carrots
1 large can (14.5 ounces) stewed tomatoes, diced
1 garlic clove, minced
1½ teaspoons chili powder (less if the spiciness gets to you)
1 teaspoon Lawry's seasoned salt
½ teaspoon Creole seasoning

Directions:
1. Put chicken, water, and salt in a kettle. Bring it up slowly to a boil. Skim off any foam on top. Reduce the heat then cover it, and simmer about an hour or until the chicken is tender.
2. Put the chicken aside. When it's cool enough, pull the meat off the bones and away from the skin. Trash the carcass and skin, and cut the meat into bite-sized pieces.
3. Skim the fat off the broth. Add the rice, vegetables, and seasonings. Cook it uncovered over a medium heat for about 30 minutes.
4. Add the chicken. Simmer for 30 more minutes or so until vegetables are tender.

10 servings (about 2½ quarts, depending on how much you cook it down).

ABOUT THE AUTHORS

USA Today bestselling authors Sally J. Smith and Jean Steffens are partners in crime—crime writing, that is. They live in Scottsdale, Arizona, awesome for eight months out of the year, an inferno the other four. They write bloody murder, flirty romance, and wicked humor all in one package. When their heads aren't together over a manuscript, you'll probably find them at a movie or play, a hockey game or the mall, or at one of the hundreds of places to find a great meal in the Valley of the Sun.

To learn more about Sally J. Smith and Jean Steffens, visit them online at: www.smithandsteffens.com

Enjoyed this book? Check out these other fun reads available in print now from Gemma Halliday Publishing:

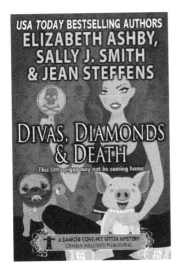

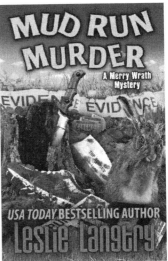

www.GemmaHallidayPublishing.com

52768744R00129

Made in the USA
San Bernardino, CA
29 August 2017